Rusty Hodgdon

MW00928200

The Subway Killer
Second Edition

Key West, Florida

OTHER NOVELS BY RUSTY HODGDON

˜ SUICIDE

A new arrival to Key West, Dana Hunter only wanted to be left alone to write and enjoy life after raising children and a divorce . But a brief argument in a bar, and the later witnessing of a suicide, lower him into the hellish depths of facing murder charges and police corruption from which only a good lawyer and the love of a woman can resurrect him.

˜ INSANITY

The denizens of a small town in California start engaging in strange, aberrant behavior. When a young health inspector begins to discover the cause in the spillage of an hallucinogetic chemical into the town's water supply, his efforts to disclose that fact expose him to possible fatal retribution.

COMING:

˜ THE EYE

PROLOGUE

She was flattered when the good-looking couple sat next to her on the subway and struck up a conversation. The female counterpart was knock-down gorgeous, and carried herself like a professional model.The guy was nattily dressed in a light green silk sports coat and dark slacks, and with his articulate and persuasive speech, looked and sounded the part of an agent. And as he carried a black leather case which obviously housed a very expensive camera, she guessed he might occupy the dual role of a photographer. The only incongruity was their mixed race.

So she was not surprised when the talk turned to modeling. She herself had at times dabbled in it. Everyone told her she was very pretty. After five or ten minutes of pleasant conversation, she felt as if she had known the pair all her life. She genuinely liked them.

Thus she was not that uncomfortable when they suggested they go somewhere to take some pictures of her. Nothing racy. Just to see how they would come out and whether or not they could help her make some good money on the side. They had contacts. How about her place?

One can only imagine that nanosecond when she knew, with a certainty never held before, that she had just made the biggest mistake of her entire life. Moments after entering her apartment, she was grabbed from behind, a strong hand stifling any possible screams. Thrown on her bed while the seeming model tied a handkerchief tightly around her mouth. Her hands were then harshly bound behind her with duct tape brought out of the camera bag. She struggled violently, but to no avail, as the man tore off her clothing, and violently raped her in the presence of the other woman. Her last living sightline was horizontally across the bed at the woman pleasuring herself passionately with a dildo as her breath was squeezed out of her by her own nylon.

Chapter 1

It's been thirty-four years. I've never written a word about it. Refuse to even talk about it. Have been denied parole twice because of that. Until two months ago. The events came cascading into my consciousness. I had to write them down. The facts as I lived them, and also as I imagined them. Not to excuse myself. Not to slant things in my favor. It's just if I don't do it I'll go nuts, and kill myself. It's that simple.

Chapter 2.

The day did not portend well. A freak, early fall thunderstorm had stripped the trees before their time, and broken branches skewered the landscape. A damp, smoky odor filled the air. The wind still blew sharp pellets of icy rain. I was on a winding rural road, when a doe suddenly leaped a stone wall into my path, forcing me to brake hard and swerve to the left. Her eyes were wild, panic stricken; the sweat glistened on her hide. Her fear was so palpable, it became my fear: I could almost smell it. She ran straight down the center of the road in front of me. It was only then that I saw the three smaller deer, one with barely protruding antlers, running about fifty yards ahead of the doe, their hooves creating small sparks as they hit the asphalt. Those in front turned sharply into the woods on the right, the doe following close behind.

The scene was unsettling, at best. I should have known then that something bad was going to happen. Big time.

Chapter 3.

I was on my way to Granite State Prison on a Saturday morning in July of 1975 to visit a new client. It was the part of being a public defender that I hated the most: a two hour round trip just to the jail itself; getting in and out another hour and a half. The prison guards, despite the fact I was a lawyer, or maybe because of it, treated me with disdain. Their movements in processing me through were agonizingly slow. But more, the physical threat of the building always filled me with a foreboding. Even though I met with my clients in the attorney's room, which in reality was a converted janitor's closet, I still got enough of a feel for the prison while walking to it. Every noise was magnified and sharpened by the steel enclosure. The odor was shocking: a zoo at least smelled natural. This was an ungodly mixture of feces, urine, male body stink. The inmates were more menacing than the guards, but only slightly so.

My client was Anthony Johnson, accused of one recent murder, a Valerie Michaels, suspected of more. Our city had been victimized by a rash of killings of college age women. Each one had been raped, strangled, and found in her apartment, mostly under their beds, some under the covers atop the beds. The cause of death had been strangulation by ligature. There was the suggestion that the killer had met the women on the subway, been invited to their homes, and had murdered them there. Each of the victims had been known to have taken the underground at times close to their estimated time of death. But no one could figure out how the killer lured his prey from the relative safety of the public transit to the private confines of an apartment, especially when the bodies began to stack up and the speculation arose regarding the modus operandi of the murderer.

The killer must have been one smooth operator.

Chapter 4.

I never really wanted to be a lawyer. My grades in school had been excellent, but otherwise I drifted in relative obscurity through my education, not involving myself in any organized sports, clubs or other outside activities.

In my early teens, I fell in love with making models, beginning with fairly basic warplanes and ships, but eventually graduating to far more complex and detailed classic sailing vessels, their hulls and rigging exactly simulating the originals. I had a special work area set up in my bedroom. While my classmates vied with each other for spots on the roster of the various athletic teams, and for the hearts of the opposite sex, I labored in anonymity on my precious models.

When I graduated from college, I had had only several dates, and certainly no sexual experience. It wasn't that I was bad looking. In fact, many women seemed initially to be attracted to me. Nor was it because I didn't have a strong sexual drive. I did. But the power of sex frightened me, and I think women instinctively picked that up. It was just easier to remain uninitiated, and alone.

I decided to go to law school against my father's wishes. He was a classic Type A personality. Never finishing college, he laid claim to the dubious honor of having been asked to leave his university three separate times before he was finally forever banned. Always about women. He drifted a bit, and my first memories are of going to the two pizza places he opened and ran in town. They provided a decent income, but at the cost of sixteen hour days, seven days a week. Eventually he went to work for a collection agency, and found his niche in life. He loved bullying people in moments of financial distress. It was a game to him, to see how much he could extricate from them despite their protestations of poverty. He eventually branched off and formed his own company, which was now hugely successful. I rarely saw him growing up, and had not spoken to him, now going on six months. Not a whole lot to talk about. I knew all I would get was a glowing report of his racquet ball prowess, his incredible health and physique, and how much money he was making.

His objection to my going to law school was that I was only postponing my entry into the work arena, which was more perspicacious than he realized. He knew my propensity for procrastination and my weakness in character. But to his credit, he paid for it, and ever since I have repaid him with silence and aloofness.

Chapter 5.

`I chose law primarily because I had no other direction and I saw a law license as an easy way to jump start a career without a lot of initiative. I did fairly well, the detail of case abstracts and the regimen of legal writing reminding me of the intricacy of my models. I finally experienced a few encounters with women, but they left me bored and unexcited.

After law school, a position opened up at the local public defender's office, and hearing that the job would involve far less heavy lifting than that with a private firm, I grabbed it when it was offered to me. I didn't really like my clientele, harboring no fantasies about who they were and what they did. Most were uneducated, angry young men with whom I could not easily relate. I never confronted them on their wild tales of how they were singled out and falsely accused. I got pretty good at sensing when a prosecution witness was not entirely truthful, and enjoyed exposing the façade in court. But it was simply too much aggravation to challenge my clients, and too easy to accept their version of events.

I clearly had no idea where this acceptance might eventually lead me.

Chapter 6.

I was already irritated when I passed through the last metal detector. Didn't a law license count for anything (other than, as the old saying goes, a license to steal)? I had to put everything loose or metallic in a decrepit locker which wouldn't close properly, and then the guards hassled me about the thin case folder I carried, which contained a single police report and a pad of paper. I had heard of lawyers bringing in contraband, and a couple of real loonies, mostly attention starved women in my estimation, who actually assisted inmates in escaping. I couldn't imagine being persuaded by someone to commit a felony.

The police report had told me that Mr. Johnson, who was black, made his living as a pimp, presiding over a stable of five women, three of whom were black, and two white. One of the women, after being busted for prostitution, had suggested to the police that her boss might be the subway killer. Mr. Johnson had apparently insinuated to her that he knew a great deal about the killings, and one in particular. In fact, he allegedly supplied some details which the police believed could only have come from the killer. For example, he suggested that he had strangled one of the victims with a stocking he had removed from her dresser. This fact certainly had never appeared in the widespread media coverage of the case.

This particular lady of the night, who had been especially close to my new client, and therefore had the best knowledge of his comings and goings, also tied his absences to the hours of the murders. But the evidence was thin, as there were no fibers, hairs, or other foreign items which tied Johnson to the crimes. I thought to myself, it nothing else comes up, I have a very triable case, which is a rare commodity in the life of a public defender. I mean, most of my clients up to this point had been guilty as hell, or at least the evidence pointed that way, and I had pled out everyone I had represented.

In any event, I was expecting the worst when I entered the attorney's room to interview the good Mr. Johnson. To say the least, he was nothing like what I had expected.

Chapter 7.

Why God gave us such a vulnerable a body part as the neck, I can not say. Its relatively small diameter, lack of bony shielding, and the proximity of the airway, spinal cord, and major vessels, make it especially susceptible to attack. But strangulation is still an act of extraordinary violence. The force that it takes to reduce one to unconsciousness, and especially death, is dramatic. Even though unconsciousness will usually occur within seven to fourteen seconds, and death within a minute, the pressure needed to achieve such results is gargantuan.

Strangulation by ligature refers specifically to the method of compressing the neck with the use of some form of wire, cord or other material. Death occurs because of a loss of oxygen to the brain, which in turn is caused by a compression of the carotid arteries and/or the jugular veins, or of the larynx and/or the trachea. Attack from behind by ligature is often referred to as garroting. It is so effective that it has been used as a form of execution for centuries. In fact, the Spanish word, garrote, means rod, which, during execution, was entwined and then twisted with the cord so as to exert maximum pressure to accomplish the task at hand.

According to the police report, each victim was found distorted, their eyes open to the extreme and bulging from the sockets, their tongues protruding grotesquely from their mouths. Sharp fingernail marks appeared about the circumference of their necks. In each case the ligature, or garrote, was a woman's stocking, which, surprisingly was never removed from the scene. In the last homicide, of which Mr. Johnson was accused, a fish net stocking was used, and the diamond pattern was firmly imprinted upon the victim's larynx, which protruded out further than any other part of the neck.

In each case, it would have taken great strength, and more, great rage, to have achieved such results.

The perpetrator had to be a monster.

Chapter 8.

Anthony Johnson was sitting in a small plastic chair pulled up to a table in the center of the room. He was about my size, medium build and dressed in a light green suit with cream colored tie. Somehow, I thought, he had persuaded the prison officials to permit him to change from his orange prison garb for this meeting. Surprising, as my experience had been that no prisoner was allowed to shed the jump suit unless headed to court.

He was one of the best looking men I had ever seen. And I usually have difficulty in judging attractiveness in men. His skin had a light chocolate hue, what might be called mulatto, or indigo. His features were a delicate cross between Negroid and Caucasian. But what instantly captivated me was the color of his eyes. An astonishing aqua green, which seemed to pierce their way out of the surrounding unblemished white. Although he was sitting down, I instantly sensed that his body was coiled like a cheetah, ready to take flight. It was stillness in motion. I could not take my eyes off his, and therefore came out with a bumbling, and quite stiff:

"Aah . . . Mr. Johnson. I'm your attorney, Mark Bowden."

He did not respond at first, but spent a few seconds appraising me.

"Mark, and I hope you do not mind me calling you by your first name. You can certainly call me Anthony. I've heard a lot about you."

His voice and tone were melodious, almost soothing. I detected a good education, and no inner city street slang.

"Where from? And I hope it's all been good," is all I could come out with. I had no idea he even knew who I was. Often my office, or the courts, failed to notify defendants of my existence, much less my role in their lives, until I walked in and met them.

"It's been very good. There are several residents here who sing your praises."

I had no idea who he was talking about, especially since the only one I knew who had ended up at Granite was a belligerent rapist who had only begrudgingly accepted the deal I had negotiated for him. But I decided to play along.

"Who specifically are you referring to?

"Names don't matter. Let it suffice to say that you are known to be an attorney a client can relate to. Would you not agree?"

17.

I had to agree. If nothing else I labored to get my clients to like me because that sentiment covered my lack of ambition and my faults in advocating their cases.

"I believe I strive to maintain good relationships with my clients. But what is more important to me is for the client to cooperate with me, and especially tell me the truth."

Now I expected him to launch into a diatribe against the criminal justice system, to convince me of his innocence. I always marveled at why those accused of crimes always felt they had to try to manipulate their lawyer into believing they were not guilty, when in fact we could care less. But Mr. Johnson did no such thing.

Without my asking, and almost seeming to know it would be my next line of questioning, Anthony began to tell me about his history. He was born into a racially mixed marriage: his mother white, his father black. Mom was a schoolteacher, which explained his fine elocution; dad was a minister. They had stressed education, and my client had a good start. Unfortunately, it was short lived. His parents were killed simultaneously in a car accident when he was twelve.

He had no siblings, and went to live with a maternal aunt, the only viable option. She turned out to be the antithesis of her sister. Married to a drunk; childless and a pill addict

18.

herself; she subjected her nephew, as she did her husband, to constant, angry berating. Mr. Johnson went from Shangri-la to hell in a week.

He only lasted four years, moving first to the street, then a succession of foster homes. He started his current avocation when he was seventeen. He made no bones about what he did; he simply spoke about it as if it were one of the most respected professions in the world.

"I think you should talk to each of my ladies, and probably Lilly first. She's the most intelligent and articulate. Brandi you will find very difficult."

Brandi was the one who went to the police. All of them were apparently still residing at his four bedroom condominium in a stylish section of the city.

I asked him a few more questions about his past, and ended with an inquiry about why one of his employees might falsely connect him with a murder.

"You have to meet Brandi. First, there was a reward offered by the family (a mere $25,000, I was aware). Brandi's greed has no boundaries. But most importantly, she had lately accused me of directing the wealthier clients to the other girls, which was not true. I think she started getting jealous, and it kind of took her over. She's using this to get back at me. But I

warn you, Mark, Brandi is also one of the sexiest women you'll ever meet, and she knows how to manipulate men with all ofher endowments."

I sensed Brandi was the most important person in the case for me to speak with. I was looking forward to meeting her, to say the least.

Chapter 9.

Brandi slid out of the king size bed quietly, the satin sheets eliciting a slight rustling sound. She also dressed soundlessly. The middle age man in the bed snored contentedly, with a little help, she knew, from the GHB, a potent so-called date rape drug, poured into his champagne. The woman quickly gathered up her several belongings, and then the diamond encrusted watch and the twenty-four inch, 18 karat gold necklace she had admired on her John as she had undressed him.

I'm that good, and entitled to some tip, she thought to herself. The five one hundred dollar bills tucked neatly into her fully filled bra was simply the fee, and Bill, or whatever his name was, had not seen fit to give her more. The blow job alone was worth the extra remuneration. Brandi knew she was a specialist at fellatio. She had even purchased several books on the art. Ever since Deep Throat, there had been no dearth of literature on the subject. Brandi knew most men, especially married, had no one who would suck them off. It gave her great glee to move her full lips, expertly combining just the right hand motion up and down a hard penis, and feel the hot fluid exploding into the back of her throat. But what she truly enjoyed was the total ecstasy which imprisoned her date. She laughed at the women who claimed blowing a man was a form of subjugation of the female. Brandi understood that once she got going, no human with a cock could resist or stop her.

On the cab ride back to the house, Brandi worried about what she had done by going to the police. She thought she had clear proof that Tony was favoring the other girls in the allocation of the "marks", as he called them. She hadn't received a fee of more than three hundred dollars for a job for months before tonight. But now she was not so certain. Could she have reacted too quickly, too angrily?

All she knew was that she had wanted to get back at him in the worst way. He certainly had said some strange things to her when the news of the serial killings had made headlines: "That is something I could do," and "they'd never catch me if I was the murderer," he suggested. She also sensed, instinctively, Tony's sublimated, but primeval anger against white women. She herself was white. When Tony spoke of his mother, his lips quivered, and his eyes became hot. It was almost as if he blamed his mother for leaving him so early. Hadn't she been driving the car? She believed he was at least capable of the homicides. But she also feared he was capable of hurting her very badly if she didn't make amends.

She had a plan.

Chapter10.

I made arrangements to visit each of Mr. Johnson's employees at various times over the next week. It was difficult. They were very busy girls. Three of them – Chanté, Tamara, and Rose – I met at two separate restaurants and a coffee shop. There must be a book on hooker names just like those that expectant parents use to find appellations for their children to be. I couldn't have made them up. With these ladies, I didn't learn much. They were clearly wholeheartedly devoted to their boss. According to them, he was an intelligent, articulate man who took good care of them, and would have been incapable of such murders. I had to agree with the first two qualities, but doubted their ability to fully appreciate them: to be honest, these gals, although quite attractive, were dumber than a sack of potatoes.

I met Lilly, at her request, at the condo. I was also curious to see the company headquarters. It was located in the west end of town, a recent victim, or recipient depending on your point of view, of urban renewal and yuppie upgrade. I made my way to the fifteenth, and top floor, and realized it must be a penthouse, as no other units seemed to exist at that level.

Lilly was waiting for me at the door. Mr. Johnson certainly had a taste in women. Clothed in a pearlescent, satin robe, her auburn hair cascading down her shoulders in small curls, Lilly looked like she would be just as comfortable in an early Bogie/Bacall film as in a porn movie. Sensuality oozed from her every pore. It took a second for my eyes to reorient from her soft curves, which lasciviously stretched the glossy fabric, to her face. There they were met by hers, which reminded me instantly of my client's: an almost bewildering aqua color which seemed to absorb my gaze. Once again I stammered out my first words:

"It's a pleasure to finally meet you, Lilly. I've heard a lot about you."

"No, Mark, it's my pleasure. Tony has spoken very highly of you. Please come in."

The accommodations transcended any expectations I did, or could have had. I walked through a short hallway which opened into a huge, sunken living room. The carpet was a plush cream color, obviously of high quality. A sectional couch, with matching chairs on either side, everything in Caribbean light blues, greens and yellows, softened the angles of the room. An enormous coffee table, with a glass top that spread out before me like an infinity pool, occupied the center area of

25.

the furniture. The place showed no signs of the exhaustive search the police had made just three weeks ago at the time of Mr. Johnson's arrest.

Lilly motioned me to a chair.

"Would you like something to drink? We have most anything. And I make a mean margarita."

Every pore in my body screamed for that margarita, or anything else that might cause me to get lucky with Lilly that night. But, frankly, I was too overwhelmed by the beauty around me, and could only utter lamely:

"No thank you. I try not to mix business with pleasure."

Lilly walked, or should I say sashayed, over to a liquor cabinet to my right, and poured herself what appeared to be an expensive Cognac.

"I hope you don't mind if I have one. It's been a long day."

In my wildest imaginings, I could not conceive what a long day with Lilly would be like.

"Now what would you like to hear about Tony. Or me?"

I suppressed the overweening desire to delve into every detail of her life, and went directly to what she might know about the killings, or especially, Anthony's involvement in them.

"I've known Tony for about five years. He was the first man I ever fell in love with, and still the only man I love today. But I've learned to share him with others. There's too much brilliance there to covet for myself alone."

Lilly then proceeded to relay to me in detail how they met, how she had made a fairly easy transition to the life of an expensive call girl. Their backgrounds shared some commonality: she also came from educated parents who doted on her. But when their marriage dissolved, Lilly, then eighteen and in her first year in college, never went back. She had dabbled in modeling and acting for a while, some of it involving the removal of her clothing, but hated the constant need to market those talents. When she found the talent that really brought in the money, and realized Tony would handle the advertising, she stuck with it.

"I was wandering aimlessly, had no money when I met him. I resisted the temptation to enter into the business for a while, but when I realized the high level of the clientele Tony could bring me and how he would always support and protect me, I increasingly saw the benefits. The way I look at it, I make more, and have to work less, than the top porn stars.

You wouldn't believe the clients I have. From every walk

of life. Many names you'd recognize. Some older. Some younger. Some married. Some not. The one thing they have in common is a physical loneliness. My single men may simply be bad at meeting women, but still need a woman's touch. The married ones sometimes aren't getting enough at home. But mostly for them it's the adventure. I know men. They need adventure, conquest. I make them think they're climbing a difficult mountain when they climb me. Then the climax of attaining the summit is so much more satisfying."

I listened to her, mesmerized. She was gorgeous, intelligent, articulate. I had never met a woman like her. She continued:

"Our culture is so hypocritical. And unrealistic. Men are going to seek women, and pay them for sex, so long as our species walks this earth. Making it illegal makes a farce out of other sexual acts which should be contrary to law – rape, indecent assault, pedophilia. In fact I believe the incidence of such acts would be greatly reduced if prostitution were made legal. An outlet, a release valve, if you will. I have no qualms about what I do. If anything, I'm proud of my profession."

What she knew of the subway killings could be found in a short summary of the media coverage of them. But she was certain my client could have had no part in them. She concluded our discussion with:

"Tony has a temper, there's no doubt, but I've only seen itdirected at the marks who try to bargain a lesser price, or whose rough play exceeds his subjective view of what is to be tolerated. He's never displayed any violence toward any of us."

I thanked her for her time, and assured her I would do everything in my power to insure Mr. Johnson would be acquitted of the charges.

"Does everything mean anything, Mark?" She said in the most dulcet of tones.

"I'm not sure what you mean."

"Well, you know, if you were sure a client was innocent, but the evidence might convince a jury of his guilt, would you use extraordinary measures to make sure that wouldn't happen?"

This was a time to recite the mantra. "I would do anything that was ethically and legally possible."

As I walked out the door, she brushed my cheek just ever so slightly with her lips. She smelled of jasmine and spice, and everything ever so nice. I noticed my hand was shaking slightly with expectation as I was getting on the elevator.

Chapter11.

My visit with Brandi was delayed because of a death in her family. I decided to use the time to meet with the prosecutor and review the evidence. His name was Sean Mac Vicar, an older, far more experienced attorney than I. But he was known as a straight shooter. I had met him once at a bar association function, and liked him immediately. I was led into his small, windowless office by a rather homely paralegal. Maybe my standards had been recently raised.

"Mark, long time no see. How long has it been?"

"Hi Sean. I think it was a month ago at the association dinner. How have you been?"

"No sense in complaining. At least I'm looking down at the grass, rather than up."

I hadn't realized after my first brief meeting with Sean that he talked in clichés. After exchanging a few more hackneyed expressions, we settled down to business.

"I don't know if you realize what a bad actor you've got here, Mark. This guy is scary. He can convince anyone of anything. The word out on the street is that we may be looking at the tip of the iceberg. We think we can get a conviction on the Michaels' case, and the connection between that murder and the others is so strong, it will be just a matter of time before we get him on the others."

I felt the immediate need to defend my client.

"Sean, looking at and talking with him, I just don't believe he's capable of these crimes. And he's got some good references."

Sean choked on a chocolate frosted donut he was in the process of devouring.

"What! Are you kidding me! Are you talking about his fillies? I can't wait to get them on cross-examination if anyone was foolish enough to use them."

I decided to move off that subject. Instead I asked to review the police reports with him. There was something new. A co-ed who had been approached by a man on the train, and had resisted his increasingly forceful efforts to go with him for a drink, had provided a description that could have been Mr. Johnson.

It was the eyes that rang most true.

Chapter 12.

Even the new evidence did not persuade me the prosecution had a strong case. In fact, just the opposite. Reasonable doubt is the lynchpin of any criminal case. I could pound that concept to a jury in this case until the cows came home. Would I finally get to do a jury trial? But more importantly, one I could win? I had convinced all my clients up to now that they should plead guilty, either to the crime charged, or hopefully, to a lesser offense. Not only for their sake, because I thought the risk of a more serious conviction, and punishment, was almost certain. But also for my sake. I couldn't stand the humiliation of sitting in court with my client and hearing the jury solemnly intone, "Guilty."

I decided to meet with my client again before seeing Brandi. I also wanted to tell him about my interviews with the other girls, especially Lilly, even though I knew I would not be entirely truthful about all of my feelings regarding that meeting.

Once again Anthony was dressed in a suit, but this time a dark blue, maybe even charcoal, pinstripe with a blood red tie. How could he get these privileges?

"Good afternoon Mr. Johnson. Have they been feeding you well?"

I wanted to control the conversation from the get-go.

"Well, Mark, we all know the age-old sayings about prison food. Hopefully they've been keeping the salt peter out."

I laughed appropriately, and asked him some general questions about any communications he had had with his staff. I especially warned him about saying, or reducing to writing, anything that might be remotely incriminating. He listened with a polite, but slightly annoyed attitude, as if I were lecturing a renowned astrophysicist on the gravitational theory of black holes, and then said:

"Mark, I would never compromise our position by publishing something stupid that might hurt us. Just so you know, the comments Brandi is now attributing to me are inaccurate, taken out of context, and were said in jest after I had just read an article on the murders. She knows that, and is simply trying to get back at me because she thinks I've been short-changing her on her appointments. That's not true, and I know it's just a matter of time before she'll come around and refuse to testify for the prosecution."

I felt I had to educate Mr. Johnson on the intricacies of

33.

the law. "Well, she may be forced to testify, and if she changes her testimony from her recorded statements to the police, she, and you, could be in big trouble. That's why I strongly advise you not to have any contact with her because she'll say you threatened her if she didn't change her tune."

My client responded: "The only way she could be forced is with a grant of immunity. I know Brandi. She'll find a way to avoid the courtroom, even if it means disappearing for a while. And if found, she'll go to jail before implicating me."

Clearly Mr. Johnson had a better understanding of the legal issues than I had thought. I told him about my meetings with the ladies, and also with Mac Vicar. I also went over the new evidence, and his only comment was that at times he had struck up conversations on the subway, preferred to do so with attractive young ladies with an eye toward reinforcing his troops, but had never been too forceful or in any way intimidating. He ascribed the whole matter to the hysteria that was beginning to grip the town. I had to agree with him.

As I spoke to him, I was surer than ever that he had not committed any of these murders. He looked me straight in the eye when he spoke. I saw none of the usual signs of prevarication that I had come to learn from untruthful clients and witnesses: the slight jiggling of the legs up and down, moist palms, eyes that darted to every place but mine. But I still could not ask him directly if he did it. It was too confrontational. I'd let him say it if he wanted.

As I got up to leave, Mr. Johnson politely asked me to stay for a few minutes.

"We've been talking so much about me, how about you? Are you married, any children?"

"Not yet. Just haven't met the right girl, I guess."

When I said this I felt my client's ability to see through my words and into my heart. Maybe it was the embarrassment I felt because of my sexual inexperience. But I could swear I read on his face an eerie perception of my predicament.

He replied: "It's tough having a really aggressive, successful father, isn't it?"

This last question, although I deemed it to be rhetorical, amazed me. How could he know my father? I needed to divert his attention.

"Well, I'm not sure I would exactly describe him that way. Anyway, I spent most of my time with my mother, and rarely saw my father. I feel so badly that you lost your parents early on. That must have been difficult."

"It was, but it made me grow up very fast. I think I had

led a fairly sheltered life up until then. And I can understand your reluctance to talk about your father: I've learned most men have 'Daddy' problems."

"I guess you're right, but I'm not sure I fit into that category," I lied. "I should get going. I'll visit you again soon once I've interviewed Brandi."

A shadow passed imperceptibly across Mr. Johnson's visage. "I wouldn't waste too much time on her."

I was out the door before I thought to ask him what exactly he meant by that comment.

Chapter 13.

Brandi wanted to meet me in a public forum. Something about her not getting along with the other girls. She was still living with them, but entirely just to ply her trade or sleep. As I came to learn, men were infrequently brought to the penthouse: only the most well-heeled and reliable ones. Otherwise part of the fee was ponying up for an expensive hotel room. The usual was the Dexter, where Anthony had a working relationship with the desk staff.

So we agreed to meet in the lobby of the Dexter, a recently refurbished antique of a hotel that had been down on its luck until five years ago when a savvy group of investors had seen her potential and restored her to her former gilded glory. Gold leaf trim abounded everywhere, setting off the late nineteenth century architecture. It was now the darling of the x-generation.

I took a spot on a Victorian couch facing the door and waited. I knew it was Brandi the moment she came through the revolving doors. Mr. Johnson had been right. She *was* the sexiest woman I had ever personally seen. Although not displaying the classic beauty of a movie starlet, or of Lilly, for that matter, her full, pouty lips, robust hips and breasts, large flashing dark eyes – why, just the way she *moved* – captivated at first glance. I could not fail to notice that the few men seated in the lobby instinctively stopped what they were doing – even if it was reading a newspaper – to watch her walk over to my couch. Likewise, somehow she knew it was me right away.

"Hi baby. It's Mark, isn't it?"

"Brandi, I presume." As if I didn't know.

"Thank you for agreeing to meet me here, honey. I just don't feel that comfortable any more at the house."

"I can understand why. Have a seat and let's talk."

"I really want to talk to you and set the record straight. I've got a lot to say to you." She clearly wanted to gain control of our tête-à-tête.

I felt I had to cut her off and regain, if any was actually lost, the momentum.

"I appreciate that Brandi, but I have a method I usually follow in interviewing a witness, and if I digress from it, I'll probably forget to ask some important questions. So if you don't mind, I'd like to start . . ."

She interrupted: "Has anyone ever told you that you have gorgeous eyes, Mark? Probably a lot of women, huh? I mean, they are sexy!"

I was not immune to a little flattery, especially from this girl.

"I shouldn't have told the police anything. I was scared and mad at Tony. He didn't even answer when I made my one phone call from the station, and didn't call back for hours. Yes, he did bail me, but that was a little too late."

"It doesn't really matter to me why you told the cops what you did. I only want to know, at least at first, does the police report accurately set forth what you said to them. Have you read the report?"

She hadn't, so I gave her a copy from my briefcase. She read it and said:

"To be honest, I don't remember exactly what I told them that day, but I can't deny that this is accurate. But right now I don't intend to talk to the cops again, and I won't testify."

"The problem is, Brandi, if you refuse to testify, you'd have to invoke your rights under the Fifth Amendment, and even if you do that, they can seek to grant you immunity from prosecution, and if granted, force you to testify." I didn't have to elaborate further to Brandi what the Fifth was. She had sufficient experience with the criminal justice system to know.

"Do you think, with my testimony, and any other evidence they have, Tony could be convicted?" A brief look of panic momentarily seized her countenance as she asked the question.

"What other evidence do they have, by the way?"

I told her, and said: "Over all, I think the prosecution has a weak case. But no good defense lawyer can ever say never. No one can predict a jury verdict with absolute certainty."

"Mark, then we have to do something. I realize Tony's words were incriminating, but I also know he's incapable of committing those horrible acts. You'll do your best to get him off, won't you? I'd do anything for you if that happened." She stared at me hard and long as she said this. I didn't mistake the tenor of her suggestion.

"Brandi, I always try to do my best. And you don't have to do anything for me if we win." I had to say it, anyway.

As Brandi got up to leave, she leaned over close to me and whispered conspiratorially in my ear: "I've got to talk with the other girls. I think I've thought of a way to increase Tony's chances. I'll tell you about it if they agree." And with that she walked out of the hotel. The scent of her expensive perfume,

and her well-washed body, lingered hungrily in the air around

me. There wasn't a male head, or even some female, that did
not follow her to the door.

Chapter14.

When I arrived at the office the next day, there was a message from Sean. Something important had come up in the case. Could I stop by for a chat? I didn't like the sound of it.

When I got to Mac Vicar's office, he was at the front counter talking in an animated fashion with a rather attractive, young receptionist. By the expression on his face, I felt he was irritated that I was interrupting his discussion.

"Hi Sean. How's it going?"

He didn't respond, and motioned for me to follow him into the inner sanctum. His demeanor was unusually grim.

I sat down in his office, and at his request, closed the door.

"Mark, we have a little problem."

Now I *really* wasn't liking this.

"We just got some test results back from the lab. Seems like some carpet fibers found on the Michaels' girl are identical to fibers from your client's home. Not only that, but the carpet is shockingly expensive, and so far we've only found two stores that have sold it in this color in the past five years. And even at that, to only eleven customers. We haven't checked out all of those customers, but I really doubt any will be serious suspects in the case. Just wanted to let you know as soon as possible." He wasn't gloating, or anything. I think he seriously felt a little sorry for me.

"Do you have a copy of the report for me?"

He handed me the copy.

I reviewed it quickly. "Sean, it says here that the fibers have six points of similarity between the samples. I haven't had much experience in this, but how many points do you need before the comparison is admissible in court." I knew that fingerprints require eleven.

"Our lab guy says he won't feel confident about testifying until he has nine. But he's still workin' on it."

I felt a reprieve. "Then you really have nothing Sean. Or at least until he finds three more points of similarity."

"I just wanted to give you the heads up, Mark. Professional courtesy, and all that."

I thanked him, and left with a copy of the report. I felt sure the lab techs would be able to garner the necessary points, and I also felt that the air was slowly being released from my balloon of optimism about winning the case.

Chapter 15.

It was time to visit Anthony again. I was ambivalent: on one hand I wasn't looking forward to the tribulation of getting into the jail and having to break the news about the new evidence; but on the other I genuinely looked forward to seeing him again. Mr. Johnson, to use a hackneyed expression, was a trip. Personal, articulate, handsome, debonair, full of interesting stories. I couldn't say that about most of the people I knew.

As usual, Anthony was dressed in a well-pressed suit, beige with a dark blue shirt and pastel green tie. He looked great.

"Hi Mark. How are you? Glad you could stop by today. I was beginning to think you didn't like me anymore."

I hadn't seen him in all of three days. I usually visited my other imprisoned clients once every three weeks.

"Good to see you too, Mr. Johnson. But I'm afraid I've got a little bad news. They say they found some carpet fibers at the murder scene which match the carpet at your condo. It's not a perfect match yet, but I fear they'll establish that. It's just a matter of time."

"So what does that mean for us, Mark? Aren't there other similar carpets out there? I mean, it couldn't have come only from my carpet."

"You're right. But they found just two stores that sell this kind, and only a total of eleven customers bought it since its inception. Excluding you, of course."

"Well, it couldn't have come from the carpet in my place, Mark, or at least, not from me from my place. We have a lot of people who come in and out, if you know what I mean."

"I understand Anthony. There are a lot of 'if's' regarding the carpet. It's just that it adds another bit of circumstance to the prosecution's case. We don't want more of this kind of evidence popping up. I'm thinking of filing for a speedy trial to put some pressure on them to complete their investigation."

"I think that's a great idea, Mark. I'm not afraid of going to trial on this. I think the jury will believe me when I take the stand and deny any involvement."

I didn't want to tell him at this time that no good criminal defense attorney will ever do anything but strongly discourage their client from testifying. History has shown they invariably insert their feet deeply into their mouths. We could discuss this later.

"I know you will advise me not to take the stand in my own defense. But it will be a waste of your time. I think I have a pretty good feel for how I come across to people. I can be very convincing, especially when I'm telling the truth."

I believed him.

We then discussed the case in general, and frankly, I was amazed at the grasp Anthony had on the state of the evidence, the workings of the judicial system, and our approach to winning the case. He had been charged twice with operating a house of prostitution in the past ten years, but neither charge stuck. His attorney had then successfully sealed any record of his arrests and brief journey through the courts. Nevertheless, he had an insider's perspective on the intricacies of the system. Talk then turned a bit more personal.

"I don't think I've ever told you this, Mark. I've taken numerous courses at some of the local colleges. Mostly in English Literature and History. I don't have a degree, but would only need a few more credits to get it. Of course, I don't really care about that. It's the thrill of learning that interests me."

"No, you never told me that. Which colleges?"

He told me. Our city had a plethora of excellent

institutions of higher learning, and he had hit the best.

Anthony continued: "I especially like the existential authors: Sartre, Kafka, Nietzsche, you name it. I know that's a bit passé, but they speak to my heart. When I was a child, I guess I believed there was a God. But now I know there isn't. There is both freedom, and chaos, when one throws off the strictures of a deity. What did Nietzsche call it, the superman? What was the German word?

"Übermensch," I said.

"That's right. Übermensch. A man who is evolutionarily superior, because he has advanced beyond the atavistic need for an answer to the mysteries of death and infinity."

"That's unbelievable," I retorted. "That's also my favorite literary or philosophical genre. But I think we can pay a heavy price for our nihilism. Not believing in any moral order or code essentially means we can do anything we want."

"Exactly," Mr. Johnson said.

We then spent the next fifty minutes discussing the existential, not only the authors and poets, but our own private angst.

"I think Brandi was too ignorant to have understood the context of my remarks," he finally said. "What I was trying to say is that I think, given just the right circumstances, we are all capable of murder. When I said I could have committed these murders, I was only stating the obvious: all of us have the capacity, physical, moral and spiritual , to do it."

"I'm not so sure, Anthony. I can see anyone killing in self-defense, or in defense of a loved one. But these kinds of killings? Planned, brutal, deviant? I don't think so."

My attention was riveted by his otherwise soft green eyes, which had suddenly become cold and hard: "Mark, then you haven't truly explored the depths of your own depravity."

As I left the jail, I had to admit Anthony was far more intelligent, even educated, than I had imagined. And he had also plumbed a disturbing substratum of my soul.

Chapter16.

Over the next few weeks I had to attend to some fires in cases that had now languished. I received the report on the fibers. As I had expected, they found the other three needed points of comparison.

A week after my last visit with Anthony, I received a thick envelope from the jail. It was from him. It contained copies of numerous cases discussing the admissibility of scientific evidence, especially relating to fibers. There were also articles from various prestigious scientific journals on the subject. All were expertly highlighted at the appropriate locations.

I knew the prisons were constitutionally mandated to provide law libraries for the inmates. Some prison libraries made the local ones look bad. But only a very small percentage of prisoners had the wherewithal to do adequate legal research and writing. That is why jailhouse lawyers were a popular group within any institution. But I had the feeling Anthony had done this on his own. Those feelings were confirmed when I received a collect telephone call from him in which he asked if I found "his" materials helpful. I told him I had, and gently questioned him on the content. He was versant in the case law and scientific theories. There was no longer any doubt in my mind that he had personally researched and located the material.

I had drafted and filed the request for a speedy trial, and was waiting for a return call from two proposed experts with whom I could consult on the fibers. I didn't have much more I could do on Anthony's case right now. So when I saw a message slip that Lilly had tried to reach me, I was able to call her right back. As if I wouldn't have dropped everything even if I had been incredibly busy.

She suggested we meet again. At the penthouse. She wanted to discuss the case with me. I agreed and we arranged I would come over after dinner the next night.

It was after nine o'clock when she answered the door. She wore a shimmering, turquoise blue, silk dress, that was hemmed a good eight inches up from her knees, exposing exquisitely sculpted thighs. Her perfectly rounded breasts delicately revealed themselves through the light fabric. She looked great. My initial embarrassment was immediately assuaged when she gently took my hand and purred: "Its nice seeing you again so soon. I actually missed you. And especially those beautiful eyes." Her tone was at once both friendly and enticing.

She led me to the couch and sat next to me, our legs touching slightly. I still couldn't speak.

"Would you like something to drink? I was going to have some Chardonnay."

I regained my composure sufficiently to squeak out: "Yes, that would be fine."

I watched her walk to a hutch which housed a small refrigerator. Her butt was small and tight. After pouring the two glasses, she resumed her place next to me, albeit a little closer this time.

"So, before you tell me how the case is going, tell me a little more about yourself. Any young ladies?"

"Not right now. Just don't seem to have the time. You know, with my case load and all. As they say, the law is a jealous mistress."

"I realize you must be very busy. But certainly you can make time for a little pleasure. It's important, you know."

When she said the word "pleasure", she prolonged the intonation of the word, her full lips parting gently to show perfect, very white teeth.

"It is important, I know. I should make more of an effort to get out."

"Well we could go out if you wanted. For drinks. Or to a movie. I love to see films on the big screen, but hate to go alone. Would you like that?"

I conceded to her I would like that.

"So now that we've got that settled, tell me where Tony stands. I heard there was some new evidence that wasn't helpful."

I explained to her about the fibers, and my filing for a speedy trial. She listened very attentively, and then said:

"I know you'll do all you can, Mark. You're very intelligent and articulate. I can't wait to see you in action before a jury."

I kept mum about the fact that I hadn't actually tried a case before a jury yet, and merely stated:

"I appreciate the compliments. And yes I will do everything in my power to win the case. I really believe in Anthony."

"I knew you would as soon as you got to know him. He really is one of the most charismatic men I've ever known."

There was a brief silence between us. Not uncomfortable. In fact, I felt very at home with Lilly. She broke the silence first by reaching over and gracefully rubbing my shoulders, and saying:

"Mark. I give great massages. In fact, I was a massage therapist before getting into the business. I would really like to massage you. Your shoulders and neck are so tight. I think your work places you in very stressful situations. What do you think?"

Her hands felt great. Experienced but gentle. I had always worn my stress in my neck and shoulders. The thought of Lilly releasing that stress titillated me beyond description. So of course I said I'd love it.

She led me into a bedroom, or should I say, a boudoir. It was all pink and whites, floral prints and softness. The lighting came from small rose colored recessed lights. She opened a sliding door to a walk-in closet and brought out a square shaped padded object which she quickly converted into a massage bed.

"It's easier for me if you take all your clothes off, but you can stay in your underwear if you want. You'll stay covered the whole time. Let me know when you're ready." With that, she silently left the room.

The ambience was all sex. The room was warm, but not hot. There was a slight fragrance of musk, possibly from some incense. There were top and bottom sheets on the bed, so I decided to remove all of my clothing. Once I was covered, I called out to Lilly that I was ready. When she came in, she had changed into a pair of white short shorts and a matching halter top. Her tanned skin delicately offset her attire. Pressing a button on a recessed panel, which caused soft, melodic music to fill the room from hidden speakers, she whispered:

"Now relax. Close your eyes and think good thoughts."

I was thinking very good thoughts for sure.

Once she had carefully lathered some warm oil in her hands, and then on my back, she started on my neck and shoulders. Rhythmically. Professionally. Hard where needed. Soft where not. Sometimes a butterfly, fluttering motion over the entire expanse of my torso. Then on to my gluts. Deeply pressing into my cheeks. Then my thighs, legs, feet. Each toe. Between my toes. Deftly into my soles and heels. Tension flowed out of my body.

I didn't want to turn over for fear she would see my strong erection. I'd never had one like it before.

"Don't be embarrassed," she consoled, anticipating my unease. "I'd be disappointed if you weren't feeling it down there." She playfully gave me a slight squeeze. Then on to my chest, arms, hands, ending with a supple rub around my eyes

54.

and forehead. Finally a soft kiss on my forehead. Her lips were velvet.

When she had finished she told me to lie still as long as I wanted. I could barely hear her leave the room and close the door. I was incapable of moving. My whole body was like putty. I don't know how long I lay there. Finally I did arise and dress. Lilly was sitting in the living room with Chanté watching television.

"Hi sleepy head. Glad you could join us." Lilly smiled lovingly and patted the seat cushion of the couch next to her as she said this. Chanté looked slightly amused.

I sat down next to her. Her mere presence filled me with desire. She was all curves and soft delight. We watched a sitcom I hadn't seen before. Lilly snuggled up against me.

I awoke, at least two hours later, with a light blanket over me and the T.V. still on. No one else was in the room. I left silently, giddy with the events of the evening.

Chapter 17.

The next day I decided to visit the good Mr. Mac Vicar again. I hadn't spoken to him in several days. It was senseless to call him beforehand. Forewarned that I was coming, I knew him well enough to expect that he would make himself scarce. Sean saw visits from defense counsel as a senseless waste of his time, as usually they only came to browbeat him into some plea bargain or another. I would only be invited over if he had some further evidence against me that he was constitutionally mandated to turn over.

I was lucky to find him in his office.

"Mark. Long time no see. How's Mr. Johnson? Here to seek a deal?"

"Not today Sean. Maybe tomorrow. Unless you'll just dismiss the charges."

"Not likely, Mark. Ever. Did you get the more recent test results on the fibers? Looks to me like we might really have your guy."

"I did, but you're still going to have to convince a jury they came from my client's apartment, and not one of the many other owners of identical carpet. By the way, do you have any investigative reports on your follow up contacts with those people?"

"We haven't reduced it all to writing yet, but I've got to tell you, we believe it's impossible that any of them could have done it. And there's one other thing, Mark. Kind of bad news for Mr. Johnson. Looks like the same fibers have been identified at the apartments of two of the other victims. It's absolutely clear to us that it's the same perpetrator for all of the murders. I think that after just a little more digging, we'll seek indictments against Mr. Johnson for at least those two other killings."

"So are you telling me that if you arrested someone for one, and it was demonstrated unequivocally that he, or she, could not have performed the others, you'd have to spring him. Or her?"

"Well I know that's not going to happen, so I don't want to speculate. Let it suffice to say that it's got to be the same person."

Chapter18.

The call came in around three A.M. that next morning. It was collect from the City jail. I could not mistake Brandi's husky, guttural voice.

"Mark. Hi. I'm terribly sorry to bother you so early in the morning. But I've got myself into a bit of a pickle. I was arrested last night at the Dexter. He turned out to be an undercover cop. Usually I would call Tony. Can you come down?"

My next call was to the bail bondsman I had used several times before. He was used to being bothered at all times of night or day. He called me back within five minutes, and agreed to meet me at the jail.

Upon arrival, I learned Brandi's arraignment was set for nine at the county courthouse . It didn't take long to get her bailed, but it was five-thirty by the time we left. I was slightly amused to find that Brandi's real name was Alice Grimes. She was twenty-four years old.

As we walked to the car, I noticed Brandi was still in her uniform: very short white leather mini-skirt, black silk blouse that revealed just enough of her bulging breasts, black suede high-heeled boots. Again, I had to conclude that many men would pay muchos dollars to spend a few hours with her. In a weird sort of way, I felt privileged to be with her.

She was initially quiet, but then said:

"Mark, I really appreciate this. We all feel kind of lost without Tony around. It's been over six years since I've been arrested, and I couldn't stand the last attorney Tony got for me. Not only that, he's too expensive. I have to watch it until Tony gets out. Could you represent me?"

I knew there was a procedure I could utilize at the defender's office which would allow me to assign the case to myself. But I was worried about the possible conflict of interest, or at least the appearance if impropriety, if I represented an employee of an existing client. Especially under these circumstances.

"Brandi, do you think that would be such a good idea considering my representation of Tony. I would like to talk to him first. I can arrange for another public defender to appear on your behalf just for the arraignment. Then we can discuss it."

Her voice was uncharacteristically cracked.

"I know Tony wouldn't object. He really respects you.

59.

And I'm tired and don't feel like dealing with a stranger on this. Even for a little while. I know how the system works. The judge, based on my priors for prostitution, could increase my bail. I believe the chances of that happening are greatly reduced if you're there. I don't want to spend another minute in that shit hole of a jail. Please. Please," she enjoined. Her eyes were damp.

I couldn't resist.

"If you feel that strongly about it, I'm sure I can make the proper arrangements. I'll be there for you."

Her thank you was heartfelt, I believed, and I decided to take her up on her suggestion we go to a breakfast place to while away the several hours until the court opened.

It was a typical all night joint that had surprisingly good omeletes. Brandi had only a tea and grilled muffin. She opened the conversation:

"Any new news on the case? Does it look any better for Tony?"

I lowered my voice. I felt a little conspicuous with Brandi.

"Nothing really. They've pretty much cemented the fact the fibers could have come from the penthouse. I haven't had the time yet to contact all the other purchasers of the same carpet. That will take some time."

"But even if they came from our place, couldn't it be argued that one of us, the girls that is, or a john, did it? Tony's not the only one who's been there, to say the least."

"Well, of course. But the fibers, combined with his statements to you, and his identification by the woman on the subway, provide at least a legitimate case for the prosecution. And there's one other thing. They say they found the same fibers at two of the other murder locations. They're suggesting that Tony might be charged with those as well. The prosecutor is certain the same person, or persons, committed all the crimes."

I visibly noticed Brandi's extensive street smarts go into high gear. "So if another identical crime were committed while Tony's in jail, that would help, right? I mean, if he couldn't have committed the new one, that's a good indication he didn't do the others?"

"Yes. I would say if the cops find another corpse under a bed, of a young lady suffocated with her stocking, identical carpet fibers, and there's evidence she recently rode the train, that would be good exculpatory evidence for Tony."

Brandi's arraignment went without a hitch. For whatever reason, the prosecutor did not ask the judge to revisit the issue of bail. I drove her back to the condo. She asked me to go into the underground parking area because it would afford more direct access to the elevator. She was bushed. I pulled into a spot two spaces away. She asked me to turn off the engine, wanting to talk a little more.

"Babycakes, I would like to do more for you. You were just great in court. I could see that the state's attorney respected you. I feel safe with you. Will you continue to handle my case?"

"As we discussed, I'll have to talk to Tony. But it's a minor charge, and if he says it's OK, then I don't have a problem with it."

"I was hoping you'd say that. Please let me do something for all your effort, both for Tony, and for me." With that, she reached over to my belt, and expertly undid the clasp and my zipper in an instant. If only I had been that dexterous with the girls.

With no apparent conviction, I said: "Brandi, I appreciate the thought, but I don't think we should do this."

"Why don't you just keep quiet for a minute, and let me satisfy you."

I couldn't muster any resistance. It was the first blow job

I had ever experienced. She slowly licked around the head of my penis, the tip of her tongue making a circular motion around the circumference. Then she started to drive down hard on me, her lips full and pressuring on my shaft. I couldn't help but elicit a long slow moan. I had never felt anything like it. As my excitement grew, she began thrusting her mouth faster and faster down my very hard erection. Finally I came in her mouth with a paroxysmal spurt of hot semen.

After she had drunk her fill, she sat up slowly.

"Baby", she intoned mischievously. "That was fantastic. I didn't know you had it in you."

I couldn't reply. I simply whimpered.

"You don't have to say a thing. I could tell you enjoyed it. And there will be more where that came from."

With that, she exited my car, her beautiful, pronounced hips swaying as she walked to the elevator.

Chapter 19.

Over the next several days, I consulted with my fibers guy, and contacted all the purchasers of the carpet. The expert couldn't help me. The fibers came from Tony's apartment, or someone else with the same carpet. My telephone calls and follow-up visits to the other owners were met with some suspicion and reluctance. The police had done a good job letting them think I represented a malicious serial killer, and that they could be the next suspects if I was to have my way. Yet I had to conclude that none of them made likely candidates, or any that I could pin the crime on with a dispassionate jury. Everyone had tight alibi's that covered at least the Michael's matter, and some of the other murders.

I also had to admit that my mind, which needed no further motivation to wander, was constantly going back to the times with Lilly and Brandi. It was if my own personal Pandora's box had been flung open. But instead of evil spirits exiting, it was thoughts and images of carnality that had gained their freedom. These two girls had reached a part of me which had remained under twenty-four hour guard for all my life.

I visited with Tony again. Brought him up to date on the carpet situation. But we mostly chatted about life. His views on prostitution were, not surprisingly, not unlike Lilly's. He told me he had once tried to get a local legislator to draft a bill legalizing the profession in our state. That got about as far as the lunch Tony had to pay for at a very expensive restaurant in town just to get the audience. Never heard from the guy again.

He had a veritable library of life experiences that were so different from mine. All of his stories were told with a wit, humor and intellect that kept me riveted.

I believed he genuinely cared about the ladies. But I neglected to tell him about my experiences with two of them. Not that I thought he'd be terribly surprised.

After over two hours, and as the guards became obviously itchy to go, I got up to leave. Tony motioned me to my seat:

"Mark, I think the girls might present an idea on the case to you soon. I need you to promise me you won't be upset with it."

"Well, can you give me an indication what it's all about? How would I know now whether or not I'd be disturbed by what they say?"

"You can't and I wouldn't expect you too. I just want you to keep and open mind, that's all." His demeanor evidenced the fact that he didn't want to disclose anything further, and I didn't press it. I just hoped the idea had something to do with massages and fellatio.

Chapter 20.

My expectations were not dashed. Lilly called me the next day to talk and invite me over for another massage. I went over immediately. But this time it entailed more. After she had finished the massage, she led me to her bed, and absolutely fucked my brains out. The sex was both gentle and hot. She knew everything about pleasuring a man. Over the next two weeks, I saw either Lilly or Brandi at least every day. I started to enjoy the expensive cognac that Lilly introduced to our sessions together. Brandi didn't require any further aphrodisiacal assistance. She just blew my socks off every time. I started to let some of my appointments go. Once I failed to show up in court, simply having forgotten the date. I walked about in a haze, my spirit and body incessantly aching for more. I couldn't get them off my mind. I was losing myself to the siren song of pleasure. I knew it, and I couldn't have cared less.

On a Tuesday – I will never forget that day – Lilly and I were in bed after a little too much drink and sex. I was wasted. She began in a whisper:

"Honey, I don't want you to say anything until I've

finished. OK? Brandi and I have been talking. We think it would be a horrible travesty if Tony were convicted of anything. Prison would destroy him, and we know in our heart of hearts that he's innocent. But we know, and I believe you do too, that the present evidence could lead a jury to find him guilty.

The state has admitted that the same perpetrator committed all these murders. And if a new one occurred with the exact same modus operandi as the others, that would probably exonerate Tony. Everyone thinks the perpetrator had a woman with him when he met his victims.

We were thinking that either Brandi or I would act as that woman, and find a man who will go with us. We'll take her back to her apartment, and fake an attack. The exact same way as the others, but we won't actually kill her. The guy won't be involved in that. It would be too much to expect. We'll leave when someone, again either me or Brandi, whoever doesn't take the girl home, interrupts us by knocking on the door. We'll bring some carpet fibers with us. But we need a man to be with us when we meet the girl, and to be there during the assault. When she describes the incident to the police, it will sound like a copycat attempt, until they find the fibers. Then they'll think it's the real thing."

I couldn't believe my ears, even though I wasn't terribly surprised.

"Lilly, there are all kinds of problems with that plan. First, the guy has to look like Tony to make it work. Remember the woman who says someone looking like Tony tried to pick her up on the train. Second, she could identify you or Brandi, or at least give the cops a good enough description to cause a line-up, or photo ID, where she'd pick you out."

"We've thought all that through. You can see we're very good at make-up. But what you don't know is that I'm highly skilled at disguises. My work as a beautician led me into doing stage work, where I learned how to alter a person's looks substantially. I could make the guy look like Tony, no problem."

Now she looked at me intently, her eyes beseeching: "We think you should be that man. You've got the same physique, and I can mix a skin toner that will match exactly. I can even change your eye color with contacts. You'll wear a hat to cover most of your hair. Brandi and I will also wear disguises. Trust me, the description she gives of us to the police will be nothing like us. Nobody gets hurt, except for some minor abrasions around the neck, and Tony gets off."

A thousand thoughts rushed through my mind. The first of which was, get the hell out of there! Then again, I'd really like to help Tony. That was my job, right? And helping Lilly and Brandi was also not low on the list.

"Lilly, that's asking a lot of me. Not only could I face criminal charges, but I'd certainly lose my livelihood – my license to practice law. I'm not saying absolutely no, but I need to think about it. You say Tony approves of the plan, and my involvement. I've got to talk to him about it. Can we discuss this in a few days?"

"Of course, Mark. We don't want you involved unless you're in it all the way. Take as much time as you need."

I took my leave of Lilly after some small talk. On the way home, I tried to think objectively about Lilly's proposal. That I was even contemplating it at all scared the crap out of me. What was I doing? But the thought of wimping out on Lilly and Brandi also disturbed me. What if they stopped letting me see them? I wasn't so sure I could take that right now. I decided to think about it in the morning.

That night brought vivid, terrifying dreams. In one I was in bed with Lilly, when she suddenly transmogrified into Tony. But I wasn't especially alarmed. In fact, it was a pleasurable sensation. Then in another I was in court on some case, when abruptly the prosecutor turned to me with glaring eyes and screamed at the top of her lungs, "You're the one! You did it!

Grab him!" And with that two burly court officers harshly wrenched my arms behind my back and dragged me to the holding cell in the basement. In the final dream, I went to visit Lilly and Brandi. I found them dead, lying on the floor of their apartment. Clearly strangled, the ligature marks purplish against their soft necks, their protruding eyes staring accusingly at me. The sense of their loss to me was palpable. I awoke wet with sweat.

Chapter 21.

My fears seemed well on their way to realization. I called Lilly and Brandi numerous times over the next two days. Either they didn't answer the phone, or they couldn't talk because they were busy. Finally I decided to pay Tony a visit.

He was in a peculiarly good mood once I worked my way through the labyrinthine jail system. Once again, without fail, he was attired in an outfit that conflicted with his stark surroundings and what everyone else was allowed to wear: a light green herring-bone sports coat that accentuated his crystalline light eyes.

"Hey Mark. How's it going. Great to see you again, as usual."

"Good to see you again too, Tony. Have they been treating you well?"

"Actually, yes. After many requests the sheriff finally allowed Tamara to bring me my favorite dish, a Beef Wellington that she makes from scratch. She learned the recipe from her mother."

I had never heard of the sheriff of this institution, or any other sheriff or warden, as the case may be, allow outside food into his big house. But then again, no client of mine, or inmate within my eyesight, had ever been allowed to dress as Tony did.

"Well, you look good, and well fed," I ventured. "Have you spoken to Lilly or Brandi recently?"

"Of course." He appeared a bit irritated. "I understand they've spoken to you too."

"They have, and I want to talk to you about it. You know what they've proposed. And I just want to know if you support their plan."

Tony's demeanor went through an instant transformation that, thus far, I had not witnessed. His voice became hard, almost cruel.

"Mark. We've all had a lot of patience with you. You're a good lawyer. We respect that. But as for street smarts, you're as dumb as a rock. Tell me what you think my chances are now if we go to trial. You know and I know that the jury will primarily consist of retirees and stay at home moms who listen to conservative talk shows all day and will not react favorably when they contemplate a black pimp on trial for suffocating young white women. I didn't commit these crimes.

And if you're not willing to step up to the plate to make sure we win this one, then maybe I should get another attorney."

At least he laid it right on the line. And it was always "we", not "I". It wasn't just my client asking me to stretch, beyond any limits I had ever experienced, the boundaries of ethical, if not legal behavior. It was the team, including beautiful women for whom I had acquired an ungodly attraction.

"I take it then that you know all the details of the plan, and you endorse it. You understand that it does not guarantee you'll walk from this one, or any other prosecutions they may bring."

"Of course I endorse it. I came up with it. And I know there are no guarantees in life. But if this one goes smoothly, I have faith that I won't be wrongly convicted. But I need you on this one Mark. I trust your instincts. Lilly and Brandi are great, smart girls, but with you there, and on board, I believe there's a better chance it will be successful."

I couldn't argue with that one. They needed a man who knew the evidence against Tony, would be able to duplicate that evidence as the plan unfurled, and who also would be able to improvise knowing the intimate facts of each of the killings. I, unfortunately, was that man.

I told Tony that I'd think further about the matter, and get back to him.

Internally, I feared I might do it.

Chapter 22.

Lilly called me the next day. It was the first time she had initiated contact with me since my last rendezvous with her.

"Hi Honey. How are you?"All nice and friendly.

"Good. How about you?"A bit stiffly.

"Great! I just bought a new outfit at Lord and Taylors. Would you like to see it?"

"Underwear? Is it too skimpy for me to actually *see*." Trying to lighten up a bit.

"No silly. Its real clothes. But very sexy. Why don't you come over and take a look?"

Well, I had planned to spend all morning at the law library. I had to finish a brief that was due in court three days ago. I hadn't even requested an extension.

"OK. Do you mean now?"

"Of course. Come whenever you can." She giggled lightly at the play on words.

I was at her door in forty-five minutes. Lord's could not have found a better model for one of its sexiest products. It was a black dinner dress that literally had no back. How it stayed on her was a marvel of engineering. It clung skin tight around her curvaceous hips and ass, ending only six inches below her tender thighs. Lilly's soft white skin served as a perfect backdrop to the attire.

"Wow, Mark. That was fast. If I didn't know better, I'd think you missed me. "A wry smile was on her lips.

"I thought you'd forgotten about me, Lilly. I tried to reach you."

"I know sweetheart. But I've been terribly busy. Let's forget about all that. Take your clothes off and let's fuck."

She led me into the bedroom and slowly removed all my clothing without removing a stitch of hers. She then took me into her mouth and sucked me until I almost came. She stopped when she perfectly sensed I was going to explode. She laid me down on the bed and performed an expert striptease in front of me. The black dress came off with one, very slow pull from behind, the fabric inching off of her in tantalizing bytes. Underneath she had on a bright red bra and undies (also from Lord's?), each hugging their respective burdens – her wholesome, full breasts, and slender but curving buttocks. Light lace frilled the boundaries.

77.

She straddled me, placing my engorged cock gently into her vagina. Then with delicate, but increasingly orgasmic rotations, she brought us both to a climax. Together.

So this is what it must feel like for a heroin addict to finally get his fix after a too-long hiatus. My body glowed with satisfaction. I was hooked again.

We only engaged in pillow talk. What she had been doing over the past couple of days. The men she had been with. Her recent spat with Chanté. No mention of the plan.

When I got home I was surprised to see a brand new, astonishingly beautiful eight by six oriental rug on my living room floor. Deep burgundy counter-balanced by gold trim. The colors were beyond description. As I walked on it, my feet sank into three inches of plush comfort. Underneath it was a thick pad that added to its soft thickness. Within minutes my phone rang. It was Lilly.

"Do you like our present?"

"Lilly. How did you get in here? And moreover, this is far too expensive a rug for me to accept."

"Honey, you should know by now we have our ways. Also, it's not really enough for all you've done for Tony, and what you're going to do. Right sweetheart?"

"Well, thank you anyway. But I don't know if I can keep it."

"Of course you can, Mark. Tony would be affronted if you gave it back. OK?"

I was going to keep it. But I had a mild feeling of being violated by the intrusion into my space.

Chapter 23.

It wasn't until later that day that I got a call from Brandi.

"Hi lover. I'm sorry I've been so hard to reach. Would you like to have dinner tonight? On me. I just got laid . . . I mean paid," she quipped. "How about Jake's?"

I, of course, agreed to meet her at seven. Jake's was the place to be. A converted, small local railroad station that had been carefully refurbished. Brass trim and lighting had been added everywhere. The twelve foot high ceiling was done in a yellow-orange fresco. The tables were covered in dark blue chiffon. Crystal and gleaming silverware glinted in the candlelight emanating from each table. I thought to myself that Brandi liked nice places.

She wasn't there when I arrived, so I walked to the bar and sat down. At the end of the bar I could not help but notice a gorgeous redhead sipping a cranberry martini. My first thought was: what kind of man would she be waiting for. Certainly handsome. Probably well built, to match her style.

After about ten minutes, I decided to order a drink. Brandi had never been late for me before, and a fleeting moment of anxiety passed through me. Had she gotten into trouble with the law again?

I saw the woman motion to the bartender out of the corner of my eye. They had a brief conversation. When the bartender served my drink, he said that it was compliments of the lady, and motioned toward the redhead. I was utterly taken aback, and almost knocked over my drink. But I summoned the wherewithal to lift the glass as a toast to her largesse. I also wanted to get a better look at her. She responded without speaking and raised her glass and took a sip.

There was something vaguely familiar about her. Was it the way she crossed her legs? The manner in which she held herself high? But that latter would only be like most other beautiful women. I began racking my brain to see if I could remember if I had met her.

My thoughts were interrupted when she spoke to me in a sweet, dulcet tone, with a slight southern twang: "I guess you all is wonderin' why I bought you the drink. Well, I jus had a hankerin' to do it. Such a fine lookin' boy."

Her speech was not at all consistent with her looks. But again, it seemed as if I recognized it. I answered her with a confused look on my face:

"Well, I do appreciate it. Especially from such a beautiful

woman."

"Why, thank you sir. And the feelings are entirely mutual, I might say."

We spoke briefly for a few minutes. Her name was Tera. She was all southern grace and charm. I felt I had been instantly transported to the antebellum era.

This brief repartee allowed me to observe her a little more closely. After a few moments, I finally queried: "Brandi?"

"Hi Mark. It took you a while to recognize me, didn't it?"

"Brandi. What are you doing?"

"Lilly and I just wanted to show you how good we are at changing our looks. Let's grab some dinner. I'm starving."

As we walked to our table, I understood why I had been so fooled. The red wig was professionally coifed in a style that was totally unlike Brandi's natural hair. Instead of her full head of shoulder length, jet black hair, she now had a short, almost pixie cut. Her nose was a little more prominent, giving her a regal look. And the eyes were a very deep blue. A pair of bell bottom pants extended to the floor, cleverly concealing heels that added four inches to her height. I was impressed.

We engaged in small talk while reviewing the menus and ordering. Her relationship with the girls had improved tremendously. Tony had forgiven her. She was satisfied with the clients she was getting. It appeared Tony had no problem running his business from jail. I hadn't asked, but it seemed fairly certain that selected personnel from the institution were enjoying the free services of Tony's stable.

Eventually the conversation turned to her disguise. How could it not when I felt like I was staring at a stranger in Brandi's body.

"So you see how effective we can be at disguises. We want you to come over soon and we'll work on you. You won't believe it."

"Brandi, I still haven't committed myself to getting involved in this plan. I have a lot to lose if something goes wrong and we get caught".

"But we won't get caught. Tony's worked out all the details. He's very smart and thorough. You don't want to see him going to prison for life, do you?"

"Of course I don't. But my way of preventing that is to defend Tony to the best of my ability in a court of law. Not to engage in criminal behavior."

"But Mark, even if you do your best in court, wouldn't you agree that may not be enough? I mean, innocent people are found guilty all the time. Especially, I might add, when they're black."

"I know what you're saying, but even this plan doesn't insure Tony's release."

"Yet you did admit before that it could be a major factor in the case. Don't you remember that?"

Frankly, I couldn't remember half of the conversations I had with either Lilly or Brandi. Either too much sex or cognac.

"I did say the police are looking for a serial killer. If an identical crime is committed while Tony's incarcerated, I think it's likely they'll either have to drop the charges, or a jury will find Tony not guilty. But again, it's a matter of probabilities, not certainties."

"We all understand that. But we need you Mark. We can't get a stranger involved with this. We know you wouldn't, and couldn't go to the police to disclose the plot. Why, you represent all of us".

I hadn't really thought out the implications of the attorney-client privilege. But she was right. Even if I decided to rat out the whole bunch of them, nothing I said could be used against them because of the privilege.

"You might be right about that", I conceded. "But I won't

be pressured into doing this. I need to make up my own mind on it. OK?"

"Of course, Sweetheart. You take all the time you need. But we need to do this as soon as possible. Tony's going crazy. And you don't want to make Tony crazy."

Chapter 24.

Our food was good, the wine better. I got pretty drunk. Our talk turned to sex.

"Brandi, don't you sometimes get tired of doing your job? I mean all the different men. Some of them much older than you. Doesn't it get to you?"

"Of course it does. Just like any other job. I remember working in a factory one summer in high school. Eight and a half hours a day sitting on a stool assembling electronic parts. They gave you a fifteen minute break in the morning and the afternoon, and a half-hour for lunch. After three hours, my fingers were numb. I can't tell you what they felt like after eight. I took a month of it and walked out one day."

"Prostitution is a luxury compared to that. I call my own hours, and have risen to a level where the clientele is pretty well-off. I've only had a couple of bad experiences, and Tony took care of those guys. Never heard from them again. Also the word gets out. You mess with one of Tony's gals and you better watch your back."

"Well you know I find you and Lilly incredibly attractive," I interjected. "That blow job you gave me in the car was unbelievable. Haven't thought of anything else since then." It was only a slight exaggeration.

"Well baby, we'll have to do that again. What about tonight?"

I couldn't finish my Beef Wellington fast enough. I got the check, and at her suggestion, we grabbed a cab, leaving my car in the garage. We went to my place because it was closer. Brandi sat tight against me in the taxi, and gently stroked my thigh.

"Mark, honey," she intoned. "Do you ever like your sex kinky?"

I had heard the word, of course, but had never experienced it, or quite knew what it meant. But I didn't want to admit that.

"Well, a little. I once had a girl squirt whipped cream in my navel and lick it off." This was a complete lie, but I thought it sounded good and made me appear more experienced. However it certainly seemed to have the opposite effect as Brandi erupted in paroxysms of laughter.

"Baby, you've seen it all," she chortled. "Was it home-made or canned stuff? Did you taste it too?" She was beside herself. "Did any get on your little dickie?"

I tried not to sound offended, but it was difficult. My reddening face exposed my discomfort.

"I'm sorry Mark," she managed to get out. "That was cruel of me. I'll make it up to you later."

We managed to make small talk until we got to my apartment. I did believe she had intentionally made me feel inferior to her. Thankfully we did not pass any of my neighbors in the lobby or elevator. That would have raised eyebrows in this mostly elderly complex. Brandi looked gorgeous but the aura of her profession was not far removed. When we opened the door to my apartment, I suddenly thought: "What was I thinking?" The smallness, messiness, sheer guyness of my little bachelor pad became all too apparent to me. Clothes still haphazardly draped over chairs, tables, on the floor; dirty dishes and food out and rotting in the kitchen sink; unmade bed.

Brandy uttered a brief "Oh", and then recovering, said: "This is cute". Just like any baby is cute.

I asked: "Would you like a drink?"

"Sure. What do you have, baby?"

It took me a second to remember the contents of my sparse liquor cabinet. "I think I have some wine, uh, a few beers. And there's some rum in the cabinet."

"What color, Honey?"

"Color?"

"C'mon, Mark, you know. Red or white?"

"Well, kinda both. Its white zinfandel." I blushed, remembering my few guy friends sniggering over my feminine taste in wine.

"OK. I guess I'll have the rum then. Staight up".

I had never been with a woman who drank unmixed rum, or unmixed anything for that matter. I poured her drink and grabbed a beer for myself.

"Well, what are we waiting for Honey? Lead me to your boudoir."

She extended her hand and took mine, picked up the small purse she had brought with her, and led me into the bedroom. Without asking she swept some clothing off the bed, and pulled down the covers. Brandy liked to be in control. With a simple upward motion, she pulled off the light silky dress she was wearing, exposing an astounding body. Large, full-rounded breasts; taut stomach; and the cutest little ass God ever invented. All of it embraced by crimson red lace bra and panties, each revealing the maximum skin while still serving their supportive duties. During our prior encounters she had never fully undressed.

"Mark, baby, let's get these clothes off." With that, she gently unclasped my belt, let my trousers fall to the ground, and in seconds, had my shirt unbuttoned and off. I stood in my shoes, socks and underpants.

"Lie down Honey."

"Can't I take my shoes off first," I complained.

"Don't worry, I'll take care of all that."

I lay down. Brandy pulled off my Dockers and socks, dropping them on the floor. Reaching over to the small purse she had carried into the room, she pulled out two strips of rawhide, each about twenty-four inches long.

I didn't like the looks of this. At first I thought she was going to whip me with them.

"What are those for?" I meekly inquired.

"Just relax honey. You're going to enjoy this". With that, she deftly formed slip knots at each end of the strips, slid one end over each of my wrists, and attached the others to the short filials that comprised my bed posts. I pulled a little, but quickly realized that just tightened the loops around my wrists. I was going to object, but frankly, was turned on enough to keep quiet and see what happened next. You have to remember this was all being done by a gorgeous woman in nothing but bra and panties. Brandy pulled off my jockey shorts, exposing a very erect member.

"That's my boy. Do you like what you see?" Brandy unclasped her bra and it slithered to the bed. Her breasts were full and round, the nipples dark and taut. She sat on my legs, facing me. I closed my eyes, awaiting, as I had before, the feel of her soft lips on my penis. Instead I felt the icy sting of metal. My eyes shot open, and my bowels almost let loose. Brandi had the flat side of a straight razor up against my cock. It glinted as it caught the light from the hallway. She had a really scary look in her eyes.

"Where'd you get that"? I stammered.

"Never mind where I got it Mark. Just listen to me carefully." I struggled for a second. It was more instinctive than intentional, but quit promptly when Brandi turned the sharp edge of the instrument toward my skin. With the constraints, and her entire weight on my legs, it wouldn't have availed me of anything anyway.

"Are you finished now? I don't want to hurt you Mark, but I will if I have to. Just listen to me and this will be over."

"I'm listening".

"I need you to experience first hand how serious we are about this plan. We need you. We can't do it without you. And we need to know NOW that you're in with us."

I realized this was not the time to debate the issue with Brandi.

"Brandi, I've been giving it a lot of thought. I know how important it is. Since you've brought the issue to a head, I will tell you I'm in." I even amaze myself of my wit under tight circumstances.

"You can say anything now, Mark, but I need you to know, we mean business, and if it's not me here with a blade, it will be somebody else later. Just so you know."

"I understand that Brandi." And I did.

Brandi slipped the razor into her purse, and then proceeded to suck me 'til the cows came home.

Chapter 25.

The very next morning I found out I had been assigned to represent a guy who allegedly ran his car into a tree at eighty miles an hour. He was wearing a seatbelt, and was seriously injured, but survived. Not so fortunate was his girlfriend riding shotgun, who inexplicably was not wearing hers. She was quite dead.

I initially wondered why he was being charged criminally, until I read the police report. Problem was he had bragged to two friends several nights before the accident that he was going to "do" his girlfriend in the exact way it happened. Smart guy. Nice guy.

I really didn't want to take the case, primarily because I was still absorbed in Tony's case, and frankly, because of what had transpired the night before. But I had no real say in the matter.

The client was being treated, and held, in the only hospital in the area that was equipped to handle patients in shackles. I decided to visit him right away to get it over with. I would have rather gone to the bar.

The trip to the hospital only took about a half an hour.

The one minor consolation was that it was much easier to get through to the defendant than if he had been in prison. I only had to check in at the front desk and show my credentials. No search or anything. Note to self: try to visit clients when they are in the hospital.

When I entered his room, I was amazed he was still alive. Tubes ran from every seeming orifice; casts and bandages covered every square inch of his lower torso, his right arm, and his head. Scary machines were buzzing everywhere. I wondered if I had wasted my time coming. He couldn't possibly be able to talk to me.

I sat down on a chair, pulled it up to the bed, and said: "Mr. Gonsalves, I'm Mark Bowden, and I've been assigned by the Public Defender's office to represent you. Can you hear me?"

I did not see any indication of a response for over a minute, and started to get up to leave. Just then I heard a low, guttural sound emanate from the direction of the bandages around his head. His mouth was the only part of his face which was uncovered: a strip of light gauze was wrapped around his eyes. I also saw him motion with his one uncasted hand for me to come closer. I bent my head close to him to try to hear what he was saying.

I heard it clearly. The man said: "Tony told me to tell you. It's time."

Totally unnerved, I ran out of the room and the hospital.

Chapter 26.

I started to feel I was in the grip of powers I could not control. I really needed to see and talk to Lilly. I thought she liked me enough to empathize with my predicament. I called her. She answered on the first ring.

"Hi Mark. It's time."

"What are you talking about? Time for what?" As if I didn't know.

"Time to make a decision, Honey."

"Lilly, Tony is not rushing me. He knows what a difficult decision this is for me."

"Tony is the one who told me to tell you. It's time."

With that she hung up the phone. I dialed back several times but got no answer. I guess the gauntlet was on the ground. Would I pick it up? Or run? And if that, to where? I felt that Tony could get me anywhere. I also would miss the attentions of Lilly and Brandy tremendously. I decided to go to my favorite bar near the office to think about it.

When I walked in I was more than a little surprised to find Sean and a couple of his fellow prosecutors, whom I barely knew, having some beers. Sean immediately recognized me and motioned for me to come over. It was the last thing I wanted. I felt as if my possible complicity in the scheme was emblazoned on my forehead. I was sure he'd sense something was amiss. But I decided it would make it even more obvious if I ignored him. I walked over to the group.

"Hey guys. Here comes Attorney Bowden, the hot-shot defender of the masses," MacVicar shouted. The group turned toward me with curiosity. My face was crimson, I was sure.

"Hi Sean. Fancy meeting you here." I briefly acknowledged the others' presence with a quick wave.

"I hear you've got your hands full with the good Mr. Johnson. He's even got you representing his girls."

"Well I don't know what you mean by 'hands full.' But I did get a call from one of them who just needed me at her arraignment. I wouldn't call that 'representing'."

"Yeah I hear she's a real looker. Getting any thing on the side Mark?"

He was badgering me, and I didn't like it.

"Sean, you know that would be a violation of my ethical duty." Or should I have said "violations", I thought.

"Well, you've got your hands full enough with Mr.

97.

Johnson. He's going down. I don't know why you'd complicate matters with his girls. You're smarter than that."

If he only knew.

I left soon afterward. Before this chance encounter with MacVicar, I was moving in the direction of at least taking the first step in the plan. Just to see if it had any chance of working. And to keep my relationship with Lilly and Brandi intact. Now I felt that the prosecutorial arm of the government was suspicious, and would be watching for my complicity. It was overly paranoid, I knew. I had only represented Brandi, and in a very limited context. But I was sleeping with, and receiving sexual favors from not just material witnesses in a murder case, but also possible co-conspirators.

I decided to get a drink. I didn't want to go anywhere I might see some one I knew. I needed to try to think this one out. There was a small bar on the way home that I had always wanted to try. I went directly.

Not a bad place. Down some stairs from the street. Cozy, but more importantly, anonymous. It was not crowded, and I didn't know a soul. The bartender was friendly but kept a respectful distance, only coming over or chatting when I initiated it. His name was Stan. After my third martini, and not having figured a damn thing out about my dilemma, I became a bit more gregarious. I ordered another martini, and as it was brought over, leaned toward Stan and said:

"Sometimes this stuff just doesn't do what it's supposed to do, ya know?"

"I figured you had something heavy going on. Could read it on your face when you came in."Pointing to my drink, Stan said: "But that's about the strongest we've got. I'd be glad to listen, if that would help."

Yeah. Right. Why don't I just tell you I'm considering faking a murder to get a client off. Loose lips sink ships, Stan. How about that? Instead I said: "Thanks, but I guess I gotta figure this one out on my own. Just keep bringing the truth serum."

"Glad to do that. How about calling a friend and talking it out. You don't have to tell the whole story. Or say it's a situation a good friend of yours got himself into, and you're trying to help him out. Just enough to get some insights into your own problem."

"Thanks Stan. I just might do that."

He retired to the other end of the bar, yet he had got me thinking. Who could I call and lay out a sanitized version of the problem? I'd had sufficient booze to start some serious drunk dialing anyway. Then Emily came to mind. I'd met her at

a party about two years ago. We went out once or twice, and quickly realized there was simply no romantic attraction there. But we had continued to run into each other on and off, and started a friendship. She was a good listener. I could tell her anything. She even once offered to put an end to my virginity, only as a friend of course, when I had spent part of an evening commiserating over that embarrassing state of things. I turned her down, for whatever reason was in my brain at the time, and we hadn't spoken since. That was about a year ago. I found a pay phone and dialed her number.

I got her answering machine, started to leave a message, when she cut in live. "Hey Mark, I can't believe its you. How the hell are you?"

Living in Hell, I almost confessed. "Great! I've been thinking about you a lot lately, and finally summoned the nerve to call. How have you been?"

We spent a few minutes filling each other in on the boredom of our lives. I conveniently left out the goings-on of the past month. Finally she asked where I was, so I invited her to join me for a drink. She lived close enough. She accepted. I had no idea what I was going to tell her. But I did agree with Stan that by circling around the subject with Emily, I might get

100.

more clarity so I could make a final decision.

When she walked in, my first impression was I had forgotten how attractive she was. Emily had done something new with her hair – more a pixie cut now that better framed her small, sensitive features. She wore a loose, ankle length dress that didn't allow me to see if she had kept her cute figure. We gave each other the socially acceptable peck on the check, and she ordered a chardonnay. We engaged in some small talk until she asked me about my work.

"I really enjoy it, Em. Not too stressful, compared to the horror stories I get from the guys who work in the big firms. I guess the only stresses are the ethical dilemmas that come up fairly regularly. Like how far do you go to help a client? Especially one you think might be innocent but has a good chance of being convicted anyway." Looks like I was getting right to the point. Have to be careful here. I had not remembered to make this sound like someone else's story.

"I don't know much about it," Emily replied. I think it's just that you never tell a lie. That can always come back and bite you. If I were a judge, I'd never trust a lawyer again once I found out he had lied to me."

"I agree. But that's easy. How about taking affirmative actions – like disposing of incriminating evidence, or not

101.

disclosing evidence when you know you're supposed to. I realize that's a form of prevarication, but it's what most disturbs me. How far do you go with your actions, as opposed to your words?"

"I guess the rule's the same. Don't do anything that could get you later on. No client is worth that."

Emily was right of course. I couldn't go through with it.

The drink turned our talk to our respective sex lives. She had recently broken off a relationship that had lasted six months. But not enough drink to have me reveal my trysts with Lilly and Brandi. Just enough to brag a bit. I told her I'd finally met a gal who told me she loved me, and that I'd had sex with. Great sex. We'd called it off, but I no longer labored under the stigma of virginity.

Somehow this seemed to really turn Emily on. Maybe she harbored stronger feelings toward me than I had imagined. She moved closer to me and began stroking my thigh. Soon enough we found ourselves at her apartment. She shared a small two bedroom with a roommate, who was conveniently out of town at the time. The place was tidy, but had the antiseptic look of two occupants who spent little time there.

She didn't waste any time, and took me by the hand

102.

into her bedroom. I started to remove her clothing by unzipping her dress from behind, but she gently stopped me, saying: "Let's get these lights off first." That surprised me, because my latest exploits had been delightfully enjoyed exposed in full light. She flicked off the lights, leaving the room quite dark so I could barely make out her form. Only then did she allow me to undress her. She took her time getting my clothes off, which was nice. We climbed into bed and started the process, until I first touched her stomach area. My hand clasped a large roll of fat, and I recoiled involuntarily.

"What's the matter?" Emily had noticed my reaction.

I uttered a vague "Nothin," yet the fact was, I was repulsed. For two months now I had only experienced taut, curvaceous bodies, of the highest level of sensual attractiveness.

I went back at it, though, trying my best to get by Emily's horrible weight gain. I stroked her hair, then her pubic area, but again, as soon as my hand inadvertently strayed to her thighs, I encountered the same problem. Frankly I was amazed. Emily simply hadn't shown her added weight in her face. I couldn't go on. I realized how spoiled I was by Lilly and Brandi's bodies. I quietly got up, dressed, and left the apartment. Emily didn't speak. I felt sure she knew what the problem was.

Well so much for getting guidance from an old friend. If anything, I was even more driven not to lose the girls. <u>My</u> girls. That's how I felt now. Every pore in my body yearned for their sweet touch, their beauty, their sex. I had to go through with it.

Chapter 27.

I slept fitfully that night. In the morning, after some toast and coffee, I called Lilly. Her throaty "Hello" proved I had awoken her. Yet I had the uncanny feeling that she expected the call.

"Great until someone woke me at seven. How are you Honey?"

I'm OK. Is this a good time to talk?"

"Of course Baby. What's on your mind?" As if she didn't know.

"I've given a great deal of thought to Tony's plan. It's very dangerous for me. Well, for all of us. But I really want to help him out. I think I'm ready to go at least to the first step. Let's see how well you and Brandi can get me to look like Tony. Then let's test the waters on the subway. See if we can get any woman interested enough to invite us over. Then I want to stop. Reassess the situation. Let some time go by to see if anyone has gone to the police and identified anyone. OK?"

"Well sure, Baby. But I have to tell you that once we get started, Tony would be very upset if we quit in the middle.

That wouldn't be good."

"I know. And I'm not saying I would back out. I'm only saying I want to take it slowly to make sure it will work."

"I understand Honey. Why don't you come over this evening. Brandi will be in, and we'll commence the makeover. You'll be amazed. Say about eight?"

"That'll be good, but can't I come over earlier and play a little?" I was beyond horney.

"Let's save that for afterward baby-cakes. Let's get down to business first. See you at eight." And she hung up.

I could tell there wouldn't be any more nookey until this thing had run its course.

Chapter 28.

I showed up at their apartment promptly at eight. Both of them were in a good mood. We had a glass of wine together, and we caught up with the happenings of the past day. I told them about running into MacVicar, and my uneasiness with our conversation. I didn't mention Emily. Both girls poo-poo'd my fears about the prosecutor, admonishing me not to allow my paranoia to distract me. They had little to relate, which I understood. A recount of their day at the office would only shock me, I was sure.

We made our way into the bathroom off the master bedroom. I had never been in it, and was astonished at its size and garishness. This would have been Tony's bathroom. Every fixture was gold plated, including the piping and flush lever of the bidet, and the faucets and handles of the three sinks set into the enormous countertop. A glass enclosed shower area was located to the right as I stepped in. It had dual heads at either end, and was at least ten by ten feet. Three different styles and colors of Italian marble tiles encased the entire area. The bath, directly ahead, was elevated, outfitted with Jacuzzi jets, and would have comfortably accommodated six persons. I could only imagine what had gone on in there.

Brandi, noticing my gawking, said: "No one but Tony,

Lilly and I have ever been in this bathroom. It is truly the inner

sanctum. You are special to be invited."

I did have the impression of being around nobility. It

was grand. I was overwhelmed by the sudden image of

cavorting with Lilly and Brandy in the tub. Even the thought of

Tony joining us did not disturb me.

Lilly sat me in a chair in a well lit, mirrored station, and

said:

"Before we apply the foundation, we need to make sure

you're closely shaved. Your beard will interfere with the

application and coloration of the foundation."

Both she and Brandi placed hot towels from a chrome

box on my face, and after my beard was thoroughly softened,

began to shave me, each taking a side. I could not help but

notice that the razors looked disturbingly like the one Brandi

brandished in bed the other night. Seemingly picking up my

thoughts, Brandi said:

"Don't worry Mark. There won't be any repeat of our

last discussions. You're going to enjoy this."

After they had shaved me, Lilly began applying a pre-

foundation moisture lotion (I read the label on the tube), and then a light tan foundation to my face with a small, soft sponge.

"Tony is quite light, almost mulatto, so it won't take much to change your skin color. The key is to create the same hue and level of saturation. We also have to make your face appear slightly thinner, so we'll apply a darker color to the edge of your face."

Next was a slightly darker lip color, a light brown mascara to my eyelashes and eyebrows. Then more shading of the foundation around my eyes. Finally the girls wet my hair, placed a tight hair net on my head, and spread an adhesive over the net. The final touches were a hairpiece that almost exactly matched Tony's hair color, style and texture, and light blue soft contact lenses, that bothered my eyes for a few seconds, but which soon become comfortable.

I had avoided the mirror during the process, which took almost an hour. When Lilly and Brandi stepped back and said, "Not bad," I stole a peek. I was astounded. Not only did I look like Tony, but I gave off his aura – that first impression that is so vital when first assessing an individual's persona.

"You guys are good! This is incredible!" I didn't mention that I felt more than a little uneasy with such an uncanny resemblance to Tony.

Lilly spoke first. "Well, Mark, here's our idea. We think you ought to go out and engage people. We'll come with you, but hang back and observe. You need to feel comfortable with how you look in front of strangers. Let's see how they react to you."

"I don't know. That's a little premature. Can't I just get used to my new appearance here for a while? Maybe one of you beauties would like to fuck the ersatz Tony?"

"We don't have that much time," Brandi interjected. "We've got to get started on this right away. There will plenty of time for great sex when we're done. Right Lil?"

"More than enough time. Your cooperation in this plan will earn you a lot of sex points Mark," Lilly replied.

I noticed that she had a strange smirk on her face when she said this, which I could not quite gauge. However, I could tell I was fighting a losing battle. There would be no more screwing until I had completed my end of the bargain.

"OK. You guys win. As usual. Where do we go?"

Brandi answered first: "Let's try that bar near your house you've mentioned. You said they knew you pretty well. We can test your make-over on acquaintances and strangers in one fell swoop."

"That's pretty risky, isn't it? What if someone identifies me? Then my cover is blown. We'd have to abort the plan and start over."

"The plan will never be aborted Mark," Lilly said with a stridency in her voice I had never perceived before. "We've got to see how popular you are with the ladies, while still evincing Tony's demeanor. We may need to adjust the make-up once we see others' reactions. Remember. You're Tommy, and you're a professional photographer." With that she also handed me a script which she and Brandi had prepared. In it were key words and phrases that those in the film industry might use. "Study it well, Mark."There was none of the normal warmth in Lilly's words.

Looked like I was going to the bar. I wasn't comfortable with this.

Chapter 29.

McGowan's was your typical Irish bar. Maybe even a little smaller and cozier, but it still had the omnipresent odor of stale beer. Down a couple of steps off the street, one came first to the bar itself, which was separated from a seating area by chest high wooden partitions. A small stage occupied the back area, where a regular guitarist and singer regaled the customers on weekend nights with Irish tunes. It was only two blocks from my apartment, so I went fairly frequently.

I had driven separately, the girls staying behind to apply their own disguises. I went in and sat down at the bar. There were two other guys there talking to each other. I didn't know them. A few couples sat at the tables behind us. Ernie was tending. I had spent hours in deep philosophical discussions with Ernie, where I did most of the talking. He knew me well.

"What'll it be buddy?" Ernie said after giving me only a quick glance as he was washing some glasses.

So far so good.

"Guinness draft." I spoke in a deep voice that I thought might sound more like Tony, but which in fact probably sounded just like somebody trying to alter his voice. I didn't think I was fooling any one. I had decided to say as little as possible, because I wanted this to work, to get out of here as soon as possible without recognition, and on to the real thing so I could hop into the sack with the ladies.

Ernie brought the beer without any indication he knew who I was. After a couple of sips, Lilly and Brandi sauntered in and sat down in between me and the other patrons at the bar. I barely recognized them. Again, they had completely distorted their appearances while still maintaining their abject beauty. Their presence was only slightly less a disruption than a volcano erupting in the middle of the establishment. Every head turned instantly. Conversation stopped. The beast had met beauty.

After they tried to order an expensive cognac, and settled for a draft beer, Lilly turned to me and asked for a light. I almost fell off the stool. I had nothing on me and stared blankly. One of the gents on the other side, sensing an opening, I assumed, quickly pulled out an expensive lighter and lit Lilly's cigarette.

Before long the girls had the two guys involved in an animated discussion about the differences between men and women. Even Ernie got into the fray. They totally ignored me. I didn't realize how articulate and intelligent Lilly could be. Brandi also held her own. They both argued vehemently that modern women enjoyed sex as much as men, if not more, and it was appropriate for women to be the aggressors at any stage in the relationship. The men maintained that their gender did not appreciate overly aggressive women, and in fact, were intimidated by them.

An objective person, which I was not, would have deemed Lilly and Brandi the clear winners of the debate. I sensed, however, that winning an argument was not their purpose. They were out to make an impression, which they did with easy abandon. The girls consistently enhanced their points with sensual gestures, a toss of the hair, a subtle hike of the skirt, a momentary touch of the guy's hand or leg. The two men were literally lapping at their every word.

After about an hour, two girls came in and sat down at a highboy table just behind us. It wasn't long before Lilly and Brandi got them involved in the discussion. They were quick to take the female side. Tony's girls joined them at the table, immediately bonded in their sisterhood. Now Brandi turned to me, for the first time acknowledging my presence, and said:

"Hey cute stuff, you've been very quiet through all this. You're good looking enough to have an opinion on the woman's role in relationships. Let's hear from you."

I muttered a few inconsequential sentences, still unsure of what voice I should adopt, and still uncomfortable with my disguise. I basically parroted several of Lilly's points. You would have thought I was Confucious. Brandi was effusive in her praise of my wisdom, my wit, my grasp of the issues. It was so overboard that I almost laughed out loud. Lilly piped in at once, more cleverly lauding my position and me. She then invited me to the table, telling the other gals that birds of a feather should flock together.

Lilly and Brandi continued to flirt openly with me in front of the other girls. I could do no wrong. I was handsome, debonair, smart, all wrapped into one hunky package. This power of suggestion, even so overt, had the desired effect. Soon Meghan and Susan (as I learned their names to be) were coming onto me. Lilly made sure the wheels were well greased by ordering a new round as soon as anyone finished their drink.

Suddenly Lilly and Brandi announced they had to go. Something about an early morning. Brandi laid two Ben Franklins on the bar, an amount at lest twice the actual bill, and seductively thanked Ernie. His evening was made. They were out the door in less than a minute.

Meghan spoke first.

"Those ladies were incredible. I'm not gay, believe me, but I found myself so attracted to the blond one. Stephanie? If I were going to have an affair with a woman, she'd be the one. But Tommy. Do you think they were prostitutes? I just got these vibrations."

"I don't think so. I mean if they were, what were they doing here?"

"They definitely weren't trying to score any tricks. They abandoned those guys for us in an instant," Susan interjected. "Tommy, I think they really liked you. You showed remarkable restraint with them. I think if I were a guy I would've been hitting on them hard."

By this time, with enough beer in me to sink a ship, these girls were looking good to me. I had also begun to forget who I was supposed to be. So I said: "Why would I want to do that? With two such other lookers sitting with me."

I frankly was amazed to see this line have a modicum of success. With Meghan especially. She started conversing with me in earnest.

I led in with my standard patter, albeit rarely successful, about my legal exploits. I had barely gotten to my representation of the subway killer, of which I guess I was especially proud, when Meghan queried: "I thought you said you were a photographer. What's with the lawyer crap?"

I barely hesitated. I was getting good at this. Or so I thought.

"I know how people feel about lawyers now-a-days. So I usually begin as an artist. I've always loved photography, cinema. In fact my brother teaches film at a prestigious college out in the mid-west. I've always been jealous of his aesthetic success. So I don't admit I'm a lawyer until I have to."

Megan seemed satisfied with this excuse. God how some people are desperate.

Before the night was out, she had written her phone number on a coaster and handed it to me. I was so full of myself with my exploits with the girls, at another time I would have asked her back to my place. Some atavistic sense of my predicament is only what prevented me. An image of my make-up melting in the heat of passion was sufficient to sober anyone. So I made my exit gracefully. I promised to call her.

As I was leaving, in fact, just as I was at the door, I heard Ernie say something. When I looked back to see if he was talking to me, he was looking downward at the glasses he was washing. On my way home, his words came back to me.

Was it: "That was a lark?" Or did he say "That was Mark?" The first did not seem like something Ernie would say. But it certainly was unusual for that bar to host the likes of Lilly and Brandy. If he had said my name, I think I would have known. I felt very nervous. I thought my disguise had worked wonderfully. Now I wasn't so sure.

Chapter 30.

The girls wasted no time in moving on to the next stage. I got a call at work the next day from Lilly, even though I had asked both of them not to phone me there. She told me to be at their place at 6:00 sharp. We were going out on the subway to do a trial run. I tried to beg off. My nerves were still frayed from the night before. But there was no dodging the girls at this point. I showed up two minutes early.

Once again, Lilly and Brandy worked their magic on me. This time, though, the job was even more impressive. Not a detail was spared in transforming me into a Tony look-alike. At the same time, they went over the script they had given me last night. Each also prepared her own disguise while the other attended to me.

"The key, Mark, is to appeal to their vanity. All women love to think they could be models. Most love to be photographed. We are presenting a real opportunity to them here. The prospect of a free photo spread will be enticing to anyone. We need to appear easy going and laid back, but also need to be forceful when necessary. It's all about closing the deal. We'll suggest their place because that will be less threatening. Lighting and backdrops will not be a factor at this stage. We're only looking to do an informal shoot to see how photogenic they are. We can either go back with them, or meet up later. Going with them is best because we can handle any last minute jitters or cold feet on their part. Just follow my lead and try not to blow it."

"How far are we going this time?" I queried. "If we can find one to take us home, what'll we do? I'm not at all ready to go any farther."

"Right. Not tonight. We still need to go over and practice the steps we'll take when we're ready. Just try to get them to invite us to their house. Take a few shots. It's 35 millimeter so we'll have to go back and develop the film. Of course we'll never do that. The first one is purely a dry run."

We walked from Tony's place to the nearest underground station, a distance of only a few blocks. Lilly wore, uncharacteristically, a pair of slightly ripped jeans and a peasant blouse. She still looked gorgeous, but like any typical college girl in town. Brandi, similarly dressed down, followed about ten yards behind, to observe only, as I was told. We hopped on the first train. Its destination was unimportant. It was already eight o'clock in the evening on a weekday, but this was a college town, and there were still a number of young females riding the rails.

As we entered the car, I noticed Lilly scan quickly around, then take a seat next to a girl in her early twenties. I sat next to Lilly. The young lady had an open, clean look. Not beautiful, but she had potential. I carried the camera conspicuously in a brown leather case. Within a few minutes Lilly had struck up a conversation with the girl. Lilly was disarmingly friendly, able to quickly engage her. The talk turned to photography, and Lilly off-handedly introduced me. We loved to meet people and show them their real self. We were good at it. Everyone had a pearl hidden inside that could be revealed by a skilled photographer. On and on. Sweetly. I saw the target was enthralled. At the next stop, however, she quickly got up, saying she had almost missed her stop because she was so interested in what we were saying. Apologizing for having to abandon us so perfunctorily, she left the car.

I could see this was not going to be as easy as I had hoped. We got off at the next stop, and headed in the opposite direction. We did this for two hours, when I suggested we quit for the night and start anew on a different day. Lilly said we were going to try once more.

We entered a different train, and again she sat down next to a young woman. A similar dialogue commenced.

121.

Before long all three of us were into it. She was Sally Monroe, attended one of the local universities, and was better looking than any we had seen thus far. Sally invited us to continue the discussions at her favorite coffee shop near her apartment. We got off at the next stop and walked to it. After a couple of expresso's, she asked us if we'd like to come over, take a few photos of her, and smoke a joint. I was getting good at this.

Back at her place, which was up four fights of stairs and sparsely decorated with an old couch covered by an Indian spread and a couple of old chairs and tables, I set up my camera on a tripod, and turned on a lamp next to the couch. Sally sat under the lamp and I nonchalantly snapped about a dozen shots. I almost felt like a pro. The mood was light and playful.

Lilly asked where the bathroom was and left the room. Sally and I began joking and having some fun together. She was witty, intelligent and honest. I kind of liked her. I wasn't keenly aware of how long Lilly was away, but thought it was longer than a quick potty run. Suddenly Lilly appeared in the doorway and asked Sally if there was any more toilet paper.

As Sally walked by Lilly to get some, Lilly suddenly swung her arm around and hit Sally on the side of her head with a black object. Sally went down with a thud. I actually cried out with surprise. The unanticipated violence of the act made me instantly nauseous. Lilly had hit her <u>hard</u>. Blood slowly trickled to the floor from a large gash on Sally's scalp. Before I could speak, Lilly went to the front door, opened it, and let Brandi in. I hadn't even noticed Brandi had continued to follow us.

Lilly handed Brandi a woman's stocking. Now I knew why Lilly had taken so long in the bathroom. Brandi got behind Sally, kneeled on her back, expertly wrapped the stocking around each of her own hands and around Sally's neck, and began squeezing the life out of her. The whole process, from Lilly hitting Sally, and Brandy suffocating her, had taken no more than a minute. I was frozen momentarily to the spot where I was standing.

After a few more seconds, I realized this was no practice run. I instinctively ran toward Brandi to pull her off the girl. As I approached, Lilly brandished a sinister looking black jack. So that's what she used on Sally, I thought. I had no doubt she would use it on me if I attempted to interfere.

What happened next seemed like an eternity, but probably took no more than a few seconds. Sally began uttering a horrible, animal like squeal, the most that could escape through her restricted airway. Her whole body repeatedly convulsed. A death pallor crept steadily across her face. Lilly eventually bent over and placed a finger on Sally's neck. Within moments she nodded and Brandi stood up. I noticed her hands and wrists were bright red from the struggle.

I had never been so torn with differing emotions. At first I wanted to run to Sally, to check to see if I could help her. But I didn't dare attempt to run the gauntlet of Lilly and Brandy. Next I wanted to attack the two girls, punish them for deceiving me. Instead, Brandi abruptly said to me: "Mark. Get the hell out of here. Now! We're going to clean up here. And sweetheart, you know better than to say anything to anyone about this."

I did what I was told. I was too much in shock to have any will power of my own. As I ran down the stairs, two other occupants of the building were at their open doors eyeing me. Had they heard what had gone on upstairs? I didn't think so. There really had been very little noise, it had been done so quickly.

When I got home, I was shaking, uncontrollably, and finally began sobbing. What had I gotten myself into? The sight of Sally's contorted face, the sounds of her death throes, remained etched in my consciousness.

Chapter 31.

I didn't go to work the next day. Called in sick. I could barely move. By early afternoon the murder was all over the local news. I couldn't believe they had found the body so quickly. Apparently a neighbor, maybe one I had seen, became suspicious and called the cops. When they couldn't get a response, even though the lights were on and Sally had been seen entering the building, they called the property manager who let them in. No further details were available. I started calling Tony's place right away. I called on and off all day. Never got a return call.

The next day, as more information began leaking to the press, I was visited by several colleagues at my office. They were familiar with the Johnson case, and couldn't believe their ears. Sam, the first to come, said he had heard they found the same carpet fibers at the scene. Henry, later on, related he read that several witnesses had described seeing Sally with a man that closely resembled Anthony Johnson. By the end of the day, the picture was clear. The killing was a copycat of the abominations that had cursed the city for the past several months: the victim was known to have been riding the subway on the day of her murder; was seen in the presence of a light skinned black fitting the descriptions previously given to the police; was throttled in her own apartment with a stocking removed from her bureau; and forensics confirmed that similar evidence was found at the scene.

I received a collect call from Tony on the second day. He had to see me immediately. Word travelled fast, even in the prison system. I had no excuse not to visit him, even though it was the last thing in the world I wanted to do.

It took the obligatory and unnecessary time for me to get through security. Was it my imagination, or did the guards perceive me with a little more suspicion than normal? When I got to the attorney's room, Tony was waiting for me. He wasn't smiling. Of course he was still dressed to the nines.

"Mark. Let's get right down to it. The word out there is that a new murder was committed. Just like the other ones. And I was wasting away in here when it happened. What do you know about it?"

"Only what I've read in the paper, or heard on the news," I lied. It's amazing when you converse with someone on this level. They know you know, and you know they know.

"Well everything I've heard tells me it's an identical crime. Plus I couldn't have committed it. I demand that you get us into court immediately and get the charges against me dismissed."

"Tony, it's not going to be quite that easy. We've still got Brandi's statements to the police. And the carpet does match yours."

"That's what you're hired to get around. It should be a no-brainer. As I said before, you really don't have to worry about Brandi. She'll never testify against me."

I didn't waste my time to explain again that Brandi could be forced to testify with a grant of immunity. I was going to have to file a motion to dismiss the charges.

Chapter 32.

Which is what I did two days afterward. I obtained all of the police reports from the recent murder, and simply used the information as fodder against the prosecution. All of the killings were obviously committed by the same perpetrator. It couldn't be Anthony Johnson because he was in jail at the time of the last one. The case against Johnson had been weak from the beginning. The accusations levied against him by Brandi came from a disgruntled employee who subsequently disavowed her statements and made it clear she would not repeat them in court. The statements were ambiguous and subject to differing interpretations in any event. There were scores of people who had the identical carpet.

We were scheduled to be in court the next week. Sean had filed a weak, perfunctory opposition raising the few points he could. His heart obviously wasn't in it. I had not heard a peep from the girls since that night, even though I had tried to reach them several times.

The day before the hearing, I was beginning the morning by carefully scrutinizing the newspaper. This had become a habit since Sally's death. I was sure I was going to look one day and find a report of some evidence linking me to the crime. On the third page of the Local Section, I saw this article:

The body of a young female was found in a room at the Pierpont Hotel on NW 50th Street. The victim had been repeatedly stabbed in the chest and abdomen. Police believe the victim was a prostitute who was killed in the course of a sexual act. The identity of the victim has not been disclosed pending notification of her family. The police gave no further information on the crime or the identity of the perpetrator.

I had a real bad feeling about this. I picked up the phone and called a homicide detective whom I knew well. Yes. Her name was Alice Grimes. She appeared to be the same Alice Grimes that had gone to the police about Anthony Johnson. No. There were no further details on her killer.

With Brandi dead, her statements most definitely couldn't be used against Tony.

Tony was brought in from prison for the hearing. He looked like an innocent schoolboy. Gone were the expensive suits and flashy ties, substituted for by a plain, starched white shirt, black pants, shoes, and tie. He had donned owlish, dark framed spectacles to complete the image.

The hearing was short and sweet. I had no spunk in me after what had happened. MacVicar, uncharacteristically, was even more subdued in tone than his oppositional brief. So

subdued, in fact, he wouldn't even look at me. The judge, who normally would have taken such an important matter under advisement for at least some time, decided affirmatively on it in the courtroom. Charges dismissed without prejudice, which meant they could be brought up again, which was highly unlikely. A jubilant Johnson was unmanacled and strode out of the courtroom arm and arm with Lilly, who didn't even cast me a glance. Nary a thank you or hug for the attorney by either of them. Not that I would have touched them anyway. I packed up my briefcase and departed quickly.

Chapter 33.

I tried to put the entire matter behind me, but couldn't. My dreams were chaotic. Not able to sleep, I walked the neighborhood at all hours of the night. I kept thinking of Sally. What did her family think? How many loved ones did she leave behind? It made me sick.

Contrary to my normal style, especially in the past several months, I immersed myself in my work. There were many surprised people who came in and found me at my desk at nine in the morning. Of course, I still perused the daily paper exhaustively each day.

Four days after the hearing, I returned home after grabbing a couple of beers at McGowan's. Ernie was not there that night. First time that had happened. As soon as I approached the main front door to my building, I knew something was not right. The door, always locked, hung slightly open. I climbed the two flights to my apartment, and saw my door shattered around the double lock and askew. A moment of panic hit me. Was Tony, or possibly Lilly, in my apartment, ready to carve my guts out as soon as I entered? I crossed the threshold cautiously. On the floor just inside I saw a trifold piece of paper. It was a Search Warrant issued by the clerk of courts. I was certainly familiar with the form. I scanned it quickly. It authorized the police to conduct an unannounced entry and search of my apartment. Now I was really panicked.

As I went further in, I saw that my place was a shambles. Clothing and dishes were strewn randomly about. The oriental rug Lilly had given me was gone. My first thought was that she or Tony had come in after the search to retrieve the valuable carpet. Damn Indian givers.

Beyond nervousness, I immediately called the detective who had procured the warrant. He wasn't immediately available, but called me back within minutes.

"Detective Howe, this is Mark Bowden. What is the meaning of this? Don't you know that I'm an attorney? I'll sue your ass off for this." A little offense was the best defense.

"Mr. Bowden." Not <u>Attorney</u> Bowden, I noted. "We would like you to come right down to the station. We've got a couple of questions to ask you. This can't wait until tomorrow."

My next call was to Sam from the office. I knew his home phone number. "Sam. I've got a little situation going on here. I can't explain the whole thing right now, but could you meet me down at the police station in a half hour? Sorry to give you such short notice, but I could really use your help."

"Jesus, Mark. What's this all about? I was sound asleep, and I've got a trial first thing tomorrow, Can't this wait?"

"Sam, it can't. If I don't go down there now, they'll come get me. I'll fill you in when we meet there. Thanks, man."

At the station we went into a small room where attorneys met with their clients. I had to make sure anything I told Sam would be confidential. I spoke first while at the same time handing a dollar to him: "Here's a buck. You are now formally hired as my attorney. Will you take the case just for purposes of getting me out of here?"

Sam took the proffered money. "I'd do anything for you Mark. You know that. But you got to tell me what's going on."

"Do you remember Anthony Johnson? The recent similar killing? Well I got the charges against him dismissed."

"Of course I remember it. I came in to see you when I read the news about that girl. And the news of your victory is all over the office."

"Well. I think Johnson's trying to set me up. Connect me somehow to that murder. He's very cagey. I think he realizes that if someone takes the rap for it, he'll never be suspected again for any of these crimes."

"What do the cops have? How are you connected?"

"I really don't know Sam. All I know is that they searched my apartment and took a rug. At least that's all I think they took." I couldn't believe that I was doing what I routinely told all my clients not to do. Lie to your attorney. Now I really knew why they did it. It's a last ditch attempt to convince someone of your innocence even though you're guilty as hell.

"Alright. But remember. Don't utter a word in there. Let them do the talking and let's see what they've got."

A detective I didn't know led us into the small, cramped interrogation room. I was shocked and dismayed to find MacVicar in there with one of the assistants I had seen at the bar that night. God that seemed like decades ago. Neither of them said hello, or gave any indication they even knew me.

Sam immediately took the initiative like any decent attorney should. "What the hell is this Sean? On what basis did you search Mark's apartment? This better be good."

MacVicar just stared at him for a few seconds, then said: "Sam, why don't you just sit down and relax. We only want to ask Mark a couple of questions. I'm sure he'll have a good explanation and we can all go home."

Sam was not going to be so easily consoled. "My client is not going to answer any questions until we hear what you've got. What was the evidence supporting the ransacking of Mark's place. You know you had to have probable cause. Tell us, Sean."

"Okay, I'll lay it out for you Sam. And maybe Mark will feel free to pipe in and explain himself. It will only do him good."

"We'll see about that," Sam retorted. I had to admit he was showing a little more bluster and bravado than I was feeling right now.

Sean continued. "We first got suspicious when we got a call from a bartender at a bar near Mark's home. He claimed he had seen a guy who matched the description he had read of the man who was last seen with Sally Monroe. He came down here and looked at the composite drawing we had done based on the description given us by some witnesses at a coffee shop near Ms. Monroe's apartment. He said the composite was a dead ringer for the guy he had served at his bar just a night before the homicide."

"Yeah. So what Sean? Where are you going with this?" At least Sam wasn't catching on. I certainly knew where he was going, and I felt like I was sinking into a bottomless abyss from which I would never escape. Why was I so stupid as to let the girls cajole me into going into a place like McGowan's disguised like Anthony Johnson?

"Well, the problem is Sam, Ernie Petroika – he's the bartender – swears that the man at his bar was in fact no one other than the good Attorney Bowden. We couldn't believe this, even though Petroika's credibility was right up there, so we tried to find the four ladies he was seen talking to that night. We located two of them. Meghan Sullivan and Susan Castillo. Never got a lead on the other two. We believe they were in disguise as well and have our thoughts about them. Both Sullivan and Castillo said that the guy they met, who called himself Tommy, initially said he was a professional photographer. Then, after a few beers, he started telling them war stories about his legal career. When they questioned this, they said that "Tommy" got defensive, and made up some lame excuse about his brother teaching film. Apparently one of the stories Tommy told them was about a client of his who had attempted to rob a convenience store and was beaten away by a grandmother with a baseball bat which she kept behind the counter. We asked around a little bit, and that's a case Mark here is currently handling. Gave the girls a lot of detail about it too."

It was time for Sam to cut in, and he did not fail me. I couldn't have uttered a word anyway I was shaking so hard.

"So you're telling me, Sean, that you searched Mark's apartment, and dragged us down here, just because a bartender and two bar pick-up's claim they saw Mark in disguise? First I'm sure it wasn't him – and even if it was, there's no law against going around in disguise. If there was, we'd have to arrest every child under the age of sixteen on Halloween night."

"There's more Sam. And remember this wasn't just any old disguise. It made Mark look like the guy who was with Sally the night she died. Not just <u>with</u> her. <u>In</u> her apartment. Two neighbors claim someone pounded on their doors that night, and when they opened them, they saw a man coming down the stairs who matched the description given us by the witnesses at the coffee shop. Which of course exactly matches the description given us by Ernie, Susan and Meghan. Ernie swears when this guy left his bar he called out to another regular: 'It was Mark!' And this guy, who was just out the door, suddenly turned around when Ernie said this. Like he recognized his name."

Now I knew why the neighbors were out when I went down the stairs. Brandi must have banged on the doors as she was coming up to kill Sally. Just so I would be seen. And why they agreed so readily when Sally suggested we go to the coffee shop. A nice, very public place, where Sally would be known, and someone would remember who she was with. But of course I could no longer confront Brandi on anything. But I sure as hell was going to pay Anthony and Lilly a call. Assuming, that is, steel bars weren't preventing me from doing so.

Unfortunately, Sean hadn't finished. "There are just two more things Sam." I didn't appreciate the smug look that passed briefly over Sean's countenance. "The poor girl had been raped. Pretty viciously. We tested the semen. It was blood type AB. Fairly unusual. You better ask your client what his blood type is. We're betting it's a match."

The thoughts raced through my mind. Raped!? How did Lilly and Brandi do it? Yeah Sean, my type is AB, and you know it is. How was I going to explain how the girls got a sample of my semen?

Sam sneaked a brief, cold look at me. Did I detect a glimpse of panic on his face?

MacVicar continued: "This last one is particularly troubling. When we searched Mark's apartment, one of the detectives was admiring an oriental rug in his living room. It

138.

was expensive, but also out of place considering the Salvation Army décor of the place. He especially noted the thickness of the pad underneath the rug. Upon further examination, it turns out the pad was really a piece of carpet, cut to the exact size of the rug, which had been inverted so that the carpet side was facing the floor. Very strange. We took the carpet to the lab, and lo and behold, it matches exactly the carpet fibers found not only in Sally's apartment, but also the ones found at the scenes of the other murders."

The enormity of what was being done to me flooded my being. I became possessed. I jumped to my feet, knocking the table askew, and startling everyone in the room. "Don't you get it?" I screamed. "This is a huge frame job. I'm being framed! Johnson and his whores have set me up. This is all their doing." I was almost blubbering now. "I'm going to go get them and make them admit what they've done." With that, I stormed out of the room and the station. I looked back once at the main door and frankly was a bit surprised I wasn't being chased.

I headed straight for Johnson's condo. I was ready to do anything to make them fess up. It took twenty minutes to get there. I was close to hyperventilating by the time I arrived. No one answered the buzzer. I kept pressing it until another resident came down the stairs and exited. I slipped by him

before the door closed. Took the elevator to the penthouse floor as I had done so many times before. As soon as I stepped out of the elevator, I sensed something was wrong. The door to Tony's unit was open a crack. He was far too security conscious to let that happen. I went to the door and yelled for Tony and Lilly. No response. I pushed the door open farther. The place had been totally cleaned out. Even the carpet had been removed, exposing bare tile floors. I wandered though the rooms, becoming even more disconsolate. Not a stick of furniture, not a thing on the walls. No indication, even, that someone had recently lived there. Nothing, until my attention was suddenly drawn to the window sill, where there appeared to be a folded note card. It had a drawing of yellow lilies on the front. I opened it. It read:

"Mark. Thank you so much for all your help. You're a great lawyer who will do anything for his client. We appreciate that. Take care." It was signed "Your Friends, Tony and Lilly."

I sat down in the middle of the living room floor and cried like I'd never cried before.

Chapter 34.

The police arrived at the apartment about fifteen minutes later. I was taken into custody, charged with the first degree murder of Sally Monroe. Bail was set at a million dollars. My father lent me the twenty thousand to hire a private lawyer. It would have been a conflict of interest for the public defenders office to represent me, even if they could have found one to do it. Apparently Sam went back and told everyone I was guilty as hell.

The evidence was overwhelmingly against me. It was even worse than Sean had laid out to us. They found three good finger prints at the scene that were obviously mine. There had been no good reason for me to be careful about that, right? Because it was supposed to have only been a dry run. Nobody was to be hurt. I guess the ladies did a rather selective clean-up.

I told the whole story to my lawyer, but there was no one around to verify a single shred of it. After several months of negotiations, during which time I became intimately acquainted with the local county jail, we worked out a deal where I would plead guilty to second degree murder, which would allow me to become eligible for parole in fifteen years. They also wouldn't prosecute me for any of the other killings. I appeared before a judge that I knew well. The courtroom was packed, especially with the media. It was a big deal to have caught the subway killer. The judge accepted the plea bargain, not without some reservations, and I went straight to the state prison.

Chapter 35.

I'm still here because I refused to admit to the parole board I was, in fact, the killer. Indeed, I refused to say anything, because I was ashamed to tell the story of the frame up again. How I had let myself be led like a sheep to slaughter.

I'll die here. I know it. And it's probably better.

About the Author

Rusty Hodgdon is a graduate of Yale University where he majored in English Literature and Creative Writing. After graduating with a Juris Doctor degree from the Boston University School of Law, he practiced law for over twenty years in the Boston area, first as a Public Defender, then with his own firm. He left the practice of law and moved to Key West Florida to pursue his passion to write creative fiction. Rusty is also the winner of the 2012 Key West Mystery Fest Short Story Contest. All comments are welcome. Write to him at RUSTY.THE.WRITER@GMAIL.COM

Made in the USA
Charleston, SC
26 December 2013